FROM THE HEAT OF THE DAY

From the Heat of the Day

a novel by

Roy A. K. Heath

Allison & Busby

First published in 1979 by
Allison and Busby Limited
6a Noel Street, London W1V 3RB

ISBN 0 85031 325 2 (hardback)
ISBN 0 85031 326 0 (paperback)

Printed in Great Britain by A. Wheaton & Co. Ltd., Exeter

Contents

For De W

BOOK 1

Pain was in the wind
Before it descended
Into the heart.

1

The Courtship of Gladys

It was February 1922, the year Georgetown witnessed the rise of a brilliant young newspaper columnist writing under the name of Uncle Stapie.

"Georgetonians," he wrote in one Sunday article, "are of two kinds: those who live in Queenstown and their unfortunate neighbours who inhabit the remaining part of our garden city."

From that Sunday the circulation of *The Argosy* — Uncle Stapie's paper — shot up, while that of its rival *The Daily Chronicle* fell.

The Davis family lived in Queenstown, in a recently built cottage at the corner of Irving and Laluni Streets. And it was in that house that Armstrong courted Gladys, the youngest Davis daughter, for six months, during which time they never once went out alone. He came three nights a week to her there and she looked forward to his coming. Her two sisters made disparaging remarks about his manners and his dress, but Gladys explained to them that he was a bohemian who cared little for these things. He was writing a book which would make him famous and they would be able to boast that he used to visit their house. They laughed at her and begged her to remember them when they came as beggars to the door of the famous author. Gladys Davis, too refined to accuse her sisters of jealousy, wished ardently that they would like him; but if they could not she would take their sneers without reproach.

"I bet he used to run about naked-skin in a village when he was a boy," teased her elder sister mercilessly, "and he doesn't say 'stick', but 'jook'. Are you sure he can read? He's probably like the milkman, who puts his tongue out when he wants to write, and lifts one foot up on the chair."

Their laugher was like barbed wire drawn across her skin; and when he came the following night she asked him to copy for her a recipe from a magazine, while she went on with her crocheting. Vastly relieved to see that he did not put his tongue out or raise one foot on to the chair, Gladys took the sheet of paper to her sisters, triumphantly pointing out the fluent, attractive handrwriting of her intended. But to her disappointment the paper did not prove to be the vindication she had expected.

"Well, can you find one good thing about him?" asked Gladys. "Is he good-looking then? Well, tell me; is he?"

Her two sisters looked at each other and then one of them said, "He's got nice eyes."

Gladys had never noticed his eyes. And in truth, she reflected when she was with him again, "He's got nice eyes. And when he puts his hands akimbo there's an air of authority about him."

When it rained and he was late she would sit at the window, pretending to be on the look-out for the occasional carriage or motor car. The moment she caught sight of his bicycle lamp bobbing up and down as it turned the corner from Anira Street she felt a sudden tugging in her throat. Then, affecting not to notice him, she would only wave when he waved first. Her cool welcome never failed to surprise him and he sometimes wondered whether she loved him and if there was any point in coming to visit her every night when he might be playing billiards with his friends. He wondered, but he came, drawn by the phantom of an eventual conquest.

Her eldest sister's favourite way of teasing her about Armstrong was to say that Gladys liked him for his patent-leather shoes, just because she had remarked years ago, as a young girl, that she would only marry a man who wore patent-leather shoes. After one of her sisters laughingly told Armstrong of this youthful vow he tried to take liberties with Gladys while they were sitting alone in the gallery. She got angry and quarrelled with him so violently he was obliged to leave earlier than usual. The next night he again took liberties with her, but this time she did not protest. Once the barrier of her upbringing had fallen she found herself defenceless in the face of Armstrong's passion. All his ruses succeeded, and had it not been for the proximity of her sisters, who were in the drawing-room, he would have attained his ultimate goal.

But on the whole Armstrong never felt happy in Gladys's

10

house. The piano-playing, the embroidery, the sketching, the genteel talk made him feel an intruder in a world to which he could never belong. Deborah, the eldest sister, had once asked him what he thought of a piece of music she had just played. It sounded pleasant enough, but he did not think anything about it. The piece had been composed by Mendelssohn, she informed him, as if she were talking about a friend round the corner. When the sisters invited him to breakfast he agreed to come, but later sent a message saying that he had fallen ill. He had had no intention of going from the start, knowing full well that at their table he would be on test. The mention of forks and fish knives, napkins and serviettes would put him in a panic and he would probably fart as he got up from the table and belch as he tried to excuse himself.

Eventually Armstrong wrote to Gladys's father formally asking for her hand in marriage; and the following night he arrived at the house to find all the lights blazing and the family assembled in the gallery to greet him.

"Congratulations, my son!" exclaimed Mr Davis, shaking Armstrong's hand vigorously and patting him on his back with his left hand at the same time. "Nice to have you as one of the family."

Mrs Davis then stepped forward and shook his hand in turn, while Gladys's sisters looked on mockingly.

To Armstrong's dismay Gladys, her sisters and mother retired without bothering to sit down, leaving him alone with Mr Davis, who offered him a chair ceremoniously and then himself took the seat opposite.

"Things change, don't they?" remarked Mr Davis, shaking his head and smiling affably. "When I was a young man the girls had to get married in order of seniority. Deborah would have had to go first. But now. . . . Foolish custom, though, don't you think?"

Armstrong nodded, desperately wishing not to let this man down.

"And your people? Still alive?" Mr Davis enquired, changing the subject abruptly.

"My father is. My mother died some years ago."

"Sorry to hear that. Any . . . ?"

"Yes. I have a sister who lives on the East Coast."

"Family," said Mr Davis reflectively. "The root of everything, I always say. On good terms with her, I hope?"

But Mr Davis did not wait for an answer, perhaps sensing Armstrong's embarrassment. "We have to treat the women right," he pursued at once. "Anyway, that's the sort of advice you don't need, I can sense."

And so the conversation went, Mr Davis trying his best to draw Armstrong out, but with little success.

Then Mr Davis began to speak of his own courting days and of the 'nineties, when "teachers did not even have a pension when they retired. Only Civil Servants did; and they were mostly white. And look at the aboriginal Indians! You have to be careful not to call them 'bucks' nowadays, and the law doesn't permit you touch their women."

Then without warning he said to Armstrong, looking him straight in the eye: "You intend to get a servant, I suppose."

Taken completely by surprise, Armstrong could only murmur incomprehensibly.

"What's that?" Mr Davis persisted.

"When the first child comes along," declared Armstrong, an unmistakable note of irritation in his voice.

"Oh, well," said Mr Davis, stretching his legs in the pretence that they had gone to sleep.

The gesture was not lost on Armstrong. Mr Davis, who had always treated him with deference, had shown his hand. You only had to cross these people, thought Armstrong, and they expressed disapproval. Let him come straight out with it if it hurt him so. Out with it! *He* was in the lion's den and he would fight. A quick submission for the sake of peace, followed by a lifetime of misery? Oh, no! *He* was not going to run his home in consultation with a father-in-law.

But by the time Armstrong got up to leave, Mr Davis's talk had set his mind completely at rest.

Their wedding was a modest affair, attended by the friends and relations of the bride; and that night the couple went by carriage to their new rented house in Agricola, a village on the East Bank, where Gladys duly delivered up her virginity on the tray of propriety, the consummation of a blameless girlhood.

2

A Buried Time

The better Gladys got to know her husband the more she missed the repressive days of her youth and the company of her sisters. The trench that ran along their street, with its green moss-like growth and stagnant water where on May nights the stars bloomed in fiery clusters, drew forth tears of longing for a buried time.

When, in the second year of their marriage, she was expecting her first child, she took on a young woman from the village, a frail but independent creature who worked for two meals a day and returned to her hovel at eight in the evening, even when there was nothing more to be done in the house. Gladys, appalled to discover that her servant had no change of clothing, ran up a dress and petticoat on the sewing-machine for her using discarded garments from the bottom of the chest-of-drawers.

Genetha was born. She was a good baby, everyone said, who dropped off as soon as she was laid in her cradle, never failed to sleep through the quiet village night and smiled at strangers who came to the house and fondled her.

The young woman, unhappy about the extra work that came with the infant, complained incessantly and often reminded Mrs Armstrong that the women of Agricola disliked doing such a menial job.

Then one morning while Gladys was pregnant with a second child, her destitute servant failed to turn up for work. Later in the day her common-law husband, a cane-cutter who worked the East Bank estates during the short cane-cutting season, came to explain why his lady could no longer continue in Gladys's employment. He came when ash from the burning canefields was fluttering down over the village.

"She couldn't come no more, miss," he said, baring his head in respect. "She couldn't come 'cause she too delicate. Everybody say that she too delicate."

"She's slim, Mr Charles," Mrs Armstrong told him, "but not delicate. In the year she's been with me she put on a lot of weight. You must've seen that yourself."

"I not complaining, miss. You treat her good; but she was always sickly. On her mother's side they does die like flies when the sick season come."

Mrs Armstrong asked Mr Charles if he knew a girl who would be willing to take her place.

"A lot of them, miss," he said, and offered to make enquiries at Diamond, where he would be cutting cane during the following weeks.

Mr Charles was as good as his word. Three weeks later he brought a message from a man living at Little Diamond that his twelve-year-old daughter would come to work for her. And it was thanks to the disappointment at losing her first servant that Gladys Armstrong came to take on Esther, whom she herself fetched from Little Diamond on that fateful afternoon. The grave child came to live in, bringing as her only possessions two dresses and a comb. Armstrong took one look at her and decided that she was reliable, even though she did not look you in the eye.

Rohan was born two years after Genetha's birth and came to carry the fond name of Boyie. And Mrs Armstrong's involvement with her children and household robbed her of the joys of recollection; and only occasionally some incident, some object, recalled a childhood experience. She would then smile and forget almost at once.

After Boyie's birth she was ordered by the midwife to remain in bed for a couple of weeks. Armstrong suggested that Deborah, her eldest sister, might stay with them for a while, to which Gladys agreed.

With Deborah came a world of scent, doilies and twice daily showers. At meal times she insisted that Genetha washed her hands before and after eating, to the dismay of Esther, the servant, who resented the new authority. Deborah even made observations on the cooking and suggestions as to how Esther might improve it.

Armstrong, as it turned out, enjoyed Deborah's presence in his home. On leaving for work in the morning he invariably asked her if he might bring something home for her from town, although these little gifts cost him money he could ill afford. Once he bought two avocado pears, and after learning that they were her favourite fruit he felt obliged to buy them as often as he could. But in the end he had to confess that they were too expensive for him; and even though she said she did not mind he was humiliated.

Despite these attentions, Deborah kept her distance. Whenever he wanted to stay and chat at table after a meal, she found some excuse to get up and busy herself with some trivial task. And gradually it dawned on Armstrong that his sister-in-law did not care much for him. He tried to put the matter out of his mind, telling himself that she would be in his house for no more than a week or so longer. In any case, what was the point in making an issue of her conduct when Gladys was still confined to her bed?

One night when he came home from work, however, the storm broke. Deborah complained that Esther was encouraging Genetha to stay up late: she should have been in bed at six o'clock. Armstrong replied that six o'clock was an absurd time for a child to go to bed and that he agreed with the servant. Deborah, hurt at the rebuff in front of Esther and the two-year-old Genetha, replied that in every civilised household children went to bed at six o'clock.

"When you get your own you can give them orders," thundered Armstrong, "but in my house the servants and children obey me!"

From the bedroom Gladys could hear the vexed voices of her husband and sister.

"Deborah!" she called out.

Her sister came to see what she wanted.

The kerosene lamp was burning low on the table at the foot of the bed and the excessive tidiness of the room bore the unmistakable mark of Deborah's influence.

"You and Sonny'll wake the baby," she said, nodding in the direction of the sleeping infant, who was lying on the bed beside her.

"Your husband insulted me," complained Deborah.

Gladys looked at her and answered nothing.

"Don't quarrel with Sonny; he likes you," Gladys then said, after a short silence.

"He does, does he?"

"Why don't you ever call him by his first name?" Gladys asked testily.

"I can't," replied Deborah.

"What's he ever done you?"

"He hasn't infected you with his persecution mania, has he?"

"Since you arrived you've never stopped criticising," Gladys observed, roused by her sister's uncompromising attitude. "You find fault with everything he does and says, even—"

"Have I ever said so?" asked Deborah.

"No. But it's in your eyes . . . and your silence whenever he speaks or I speak of him."

"Look, Gladys," Deborah said haughtily, "I won't have you talking to me like that. Your relations with Armstrong—"

"Sonny's his name!" Gladys shouted at her.

The baby began crying and Armstrong came hurrying into the room. Deborah bent down to pick up the infant as she often did during the day, but Gladys took up the child before her sister could get to it. Deborah drew back, her face contorted with disbelief and pain, while the infant's arms thrashed the air and it screamed in protest.

Armstrong gently lifted the child from his wife's arms and, to hide his embarrassment, left the room, while Deborah, in her anger, was unable to move away from her sister's bedside. But she felt equally incapable of remaining. When, finally, Gladys spoke to her, she summoned up what little dignity she had left and walked out of the room without minding to answer.

The next morning Armstrong got up at five o'clock to feed the fowls. After they had eaten the mixture of rice and corn, he caught the hens one by one and thrust a finger into their backsides to check which of them would lay that day. That done, he filled the goblet with rain water from the vat and began to climb the stairs with it.

When Armstrong was halfway up the stairs, the back door opened and Deborah appeared, carrying her suitcase.

"You're not going?" Armstrong asked, putting down the goblet.

"Yes. It's best for all concerned," she answered.

"Don't you ever quarrel in your home?"

"No.'

"Ah."

He put out his hand and shook hers.

"Would you like me to carry your grip for you?" he offered.

"Thanks, no. It's not heavy. Goodbye."

"Goodbye, then," Armstrong returned.

He went to the gate and watched her out of sight. From the cab driver's yard came the tinkle of harness as he prepared to go out on his daily search for fares. The fresh morning breeze rustled the cherry tree over the fence and brought the smell of the river to Armstrong's yard. A cock crowed from a yard deeper in the village, and its voice reverberated on the air, heady with the smell of vegetation and dew and horse dung. The cab driver had pulled out his cab on to the road, where it stood with its shafts dug into the ground. In a moment he would be hitching his horse to it and he would be off. It occurred to Armstrong that it was too early for a tram and that his sister-in-law would be standing on the Public Road for a good hour.

"Fool!" he muttered.

Armstrong drew satisfaction from the thought of her spindly legs supporting her overweight body for sixty minutes in front of the rum shop, while the village awakened. He went back to his goblet, which he took upstairs and placed on the dresser. It was going to be a hot day and Esther would probably need to fill it again.

What hurt Deborah especially was that she was obliged to carry her own suitcase to the Public Road. She had put it down several times before reaching the point where she was to wait for the tram. As she stood and re-enacted in her mind the quarrel of the evening before, the feeling gradually overcame her that yesterday was probably the beginning of a permanent estangement between herself and her sister.

Before she came to Agricola her father had warned her

18

against interfering in the way of life of the household. As things turned out this was impossible. She had taken over many of the duties of her convalescing sister and it was not practicable to enquire in detail as to how they should be done. But yesterday's scene need never have occurred. She had underestimated Armstrong, who the day before had been friendly enough. What had been responsible for his fit of temper? Her attitude towards him had been consistent and she had always made sure that Esther had a hot cup of chocolate ready for him when he came home in the evenings. What's done is done! He lacked breeding, and there was nothing she could do about that.

"Do you know the time?" she enquired of a barefooted East Indian couple who were about to cross the Public Road.

"Me in' know no time, missie. But if you waiting 'pon the tram he in' going come till sun come up good."

"Thanks," she answered.

The couple crossed the road, the woman treading in the man's footsteps.

"What did I do to offend him?" the question kept coming back to her.

And at one point Deborah felt like returning to ask Armstrong why his attitude towards her had altered.

"It would've been a place to come for a change," the thought occurred to her. And Genetha had grown fond of her. She could tell.

"But the servant needs her wings clipping. She thinks she owns the place."

An orange glow which had appeared in the sky ridged the houses in Agricola with a line of light. When the tram appeared suddenly, long before the couple said it would, Deborah just had time to wave it to a stop. She climbed in and sat next to a woman who was apparently going to market and had contrived to heap on her lap a basket of vegetables, a bunch of plantains and a live chicken. Deborah was obviously destined to travel to Georgetown with a plantain in one ear and a cock threatening to descend on her head with every jolt of the tram. The ride was not conducive to reflection and she passed the time listening to the conversation round her.

Back home she told her parents and her sister her version of what had occurred.

"I always said he was an odd sort," Mr Davis observed, sucking at his empty pipe. "Poor Gladys! And with two children on her hands. . . . Great pity she didn't marry someone with backbone — and background. Without background you're nowhere."

His wife shook her head in harmony, as always, with her husband.

"God knows best," she muttered.

"You ever heard them quarrelling?" Gladys's other sister asked.

"No. But you can feel there's something. As soon as my back was turned I'm sure it came out again."

"Poor Gladys!" repeated Mr Davis, shaking his head knowingly.

After Deborah left, Armstrong fell into a surly mood. The sight of his wife, healthy looking and in good appetite, immobile while he had to be up early, annoyed him. The midwife had prescribed two weeks' rest; but a week ago she was ill. Now she was as fit as he was. She said so herself.

When Armstrong remarked to Gladys that she was well enough to get up she said she ought to do as the midwife said, but would get up if he wished it.

"No," he rejoined magnanimously.

But the same night, on returning home after a drinking bout with his friends, he shouted at her for lying in bed like a "fat sow".

"Now you taste a couple of weeks in bed, you don't want to lef' it, eh?"

Whenever he was drunk he threw away the grammar he so sedulously cultivated in the presence of educated people.

"You lazy, good-for-nothing!" he shouted at the top of his voice. "Get your tail up an' earn you keep. You can begin by making me something fo' eat. I don't want this tripe that Esther did make here. You want to turn me into one of these aunty-men who kian' even tell whether he coming or going? Is me who got for turn out early in the morning to work for you and your children. You sister come here and behave as if she own the village. One week and she cause confusion! It's all this piano-playing and embroidery. If you pass you childhood tinkling away 'pon a piano and pushing a needle you in' going be good for nothing. You kian' even cook cook-up rice. It's a disgrace! If I sit down home and don't work your father would soon be round here telling me I married an' got to support his daughter. Make no bones about it! He would come round here and like all you family he would start laying down the law. I know your people, girl. They had you on the shelf an' was so anxious to get you off it they accept any Tom, Dick and Harry. But when things not going right they want the man to account to them."

He was breathing heavily and stood by the bed-post with a finger pointing down at her face.

"I can't talk to you when you're in this condition," she protested.

"Why the hell I din' marry a woman from my own village I don't know. One of them big-batty women with powerful build who kian' tell a piano from a violin. At least she would'a been up the day after she deliver she child, and I wouldn't have she father sitting on the sidelines judging me."

Genetha, who had come into the room unnoticed, began to bawl, and immediately afterwards the infant began to cry as well.

"You see!" continued Armstrong. "He begin again. The child begin again. I kian' even talk in my own house any more."

Gladys hurriedly picked up the baby, alarmed at his menacing attitude. Armstrong screamed for Esther, who hurried into the room.

"Take this child out'f here!" he bellowed.

Then, suddenly, he sat down on the bed and covered his head with his hands.

"Oh, God, I dunno," he muttered.

He wanted to throw himself at his wife's feet and say he was sorry. How could he explain that he did not mean a single word he had spoken and that all he wanted was to provide a happy home for his family? What force within him drove him to do the very thing he did not want to do?

The infant's wailing became a whimper and in the end gave way to sleep.

Armstrong got up and went into the drawing-room, where the light from the oil lamp failed to reach the corners. He sat down in a chair by the ornamental pedestal, in the most obscure part of the room. From where he sat he could see Esther ironing. She had given the infant back to its mother and was now tackling a pile of clothes on the dining table. From the top of the heap she took a garment to be pressed as soon as she had laid a finished one on the chair. He saw his wife go into the kitchen to prepare the meal he had asked for, but did not really want and from time to time Esther would slip off to change irons and blow the embers of the burning charcoal. Genetha, cowed and silent, was sitting in a chair at the table where Esther was ironing, her thumb in her mouth.

After putting her husband's meal on the table Mrs Armstrong signalled to Genetha to go inside and wait for her. She walked around as in a dream, wiping her hand on the corner of her dress as some people wash their hands, without any reason, except to relieve the tension in their minds. If her husband had been out she would have taken over the ironing from Esther, just to give her hands something to do for a few hours. The washing-up was not absorbing enough; embroidery was not possible in the half-light. Tonight she would find it impossible to sleep, but he would sleep like a log. He always did, no matter how badly they quarrelled. Whenever he got up to drink a glass of water or to urinate and found her sitting at the open window, he became angry and asked her if she was studying the stars. Only people with bad consciences could not sleep at night. She would then go back to bed to please him and in a short while he would be snoring again.

Armstrong ate his meal, picked his teeth with his fingers and then got up from the table to go into the kitchen. The fire was going out, but instead of speaking sharply to Esther about it he put some new charcoal on the coal-pot and replaced the irons on top. He could see the two huge pots with their blood-leafed croton plants in the back yard. Filling an enamel basin with water he went downstairs to water the shrubs and pick off the dead leaves. He heard the noise of the iron as Esther brought it down on the table and thought that he must get new lime for the latrine in the yard and send for Baboo to cut the grass, which had grown right up to the foot of the back stairs. In the end he had to go back upstairs and face the silence, broken only by the pounding of Esther's ironing.

Soon Armstrong could hear his wife speaking softly to Genetha. The gentle voice soothed his agitation. like cochineal on a burning head. When they were just married he used to play ducks and drakes in the trench at the back of the yard, where he revelled in his ability to make a mango seed skid on the surface of the water. In those days he was less irritable. It was as if a cancer were growing in his body and gaining control so effectively that he was no longer master of his own actions. He knew how to achieve peace in his house, but as soon as things were going well, as soon as Gladys began to talk a little the cancer would grope into the part of his brain that ordered his actions and would dictate an outburst without cause, when she was smiling or offering to do something that might please him. And he knew that with every outburst, with every quarrel, her silences lasted longer, so that the time might come when the gulf between them became so great that no penitence, no sustained act of indulgence could bridge it. Was it true what her family thought of him? That he was coarse? Was it really his fault that Deborah had left, without even saying goodbye to her sister? Was he wrong about her and her arrogance? He puzzled over these questions until the dull noise from the iron stopped.

3

Rohan

Unlike his sister, who as an infant slept long and fed readily at the breast, the boy-child spent several minutes adjusting his mouth to the nipple, only to suck fitfully when he had it firmly in his mouth. His sleep was as restless as his feeding, so much so that his father deserted the conjugal room in order to make certain of a full night's rest. He exchanged sleeping quarters with Esther, who had to get up whenever the baby cried and try to soothe him to sleep.

At first Armstrong made much of his son and he bought him a little shak-shak made of celluloid to amuse him during his waking hours. His favourite game with the infant consisted of picking him up in such a way that he gripped his fingers, demonstrating to his wife and anyone who cared to watch that infants had a powerful grasp at an early age.

Armstrong, deciding that the christening of his boy-child should be celebrated, invited his friends and those he knew tolerably well in the village. His in-laws were invited by letter, as a formality only, since he was certain that they would not come. But, to Gladys's delight, they came. She took advantage of the occasion to become reconciled with Deborah, who promised that she would return to stay with them another time, without having the slightest intention of keeping her promise. Alice, the second sister, admired the baby, not failing to observe that it bore a strong resemblance to its father.

Armstrong took Alice downstairs to show her the crotons and the pineapple bed by the trench. It was dark, and the rustling of a salipenta in the long grass startled her. She had never seen a lizard as large as that before and remarked that if she lived there she would make sure that the grass was kept short. They went back upstairs when the music began.

Mrs Davis wanted to see the yard as well and the fruit trees at the back, but her daughter warned her against going down, on account of the salipentas.

Alice pitied her sister because there was no indoor toilet; and when, in the kitchen, she discovered that there was no running water either, she asked Gladys:

"How d'you manage?" puckering her brows in an expression of concern.

"Sonny brings up water from the vat before he goes to work."

"Oh," Alice said, relieved.

A young man came to invite Alice to dance and the couple danced off, maintaining a distance of at least two feet from each other.

One of Armstrong's friends pretended to give the infant a schnapp-glass of rum, and though Gladys's parents were shocked by such ribaldry they were obliged to laugh.

"He just like his father, you know," remarked the friend, to Armstrong's annoyance. "He know how much liquor he can take."

Gladys's parents looked at each other, an exchange of glances that did not escape the infant's mother, whose only wish was that the evening would pass without incident. Each of Armstrong's friends danced with Alice in turn, pushing and dragging her round the drawing-room at a furious pace, in the manner of the new dance step which Alice had never dared practise at home.

Armstrong's friends teased him, saying that he was more interested in his sister-in-law than in his wife, which gave rise to a discussion about Alice's figure. Her breasts were firm, for some, but on the small side, they agreed. Her backside was too large for some, but just right for others. There was no disagreement, however, on the fact that her mouth was formed to be kissed. One of them observed that he preferred the mother, at which they all burst out laughing. They then turned to the other women in the drawing-room, rejecting some as hopeless specimens and admitting others as a fit subject for discussion.

From time to time Armstrong went over to his wife, who was sitting in a corner with the infant on her lap, apparently unmindful of the noise around him.

At ten o'clock the table on which the cake stood was dragged to the centre of the room, where everyone gathered round it. Armstrong's father-in-law, who was adjudged the most educated man present, was asked to make the speech. He cleared his throat, paused for a suitable length of time and then began. A child was born into the world, he said. The next few years would probably be his happiest, when all the best things would come to him at no cost in money or anxiety. (At this point there was a groan of approval from the women present.) Later, he went on, when he started to earn his living, when he married and had to maintain a household, perhaps two — and here there was a roar of laughter from the men and scowls from the women — he would come to know the other side of life, the uncertainties, the wanting, the pain of unfulfilled hopes.

"And it all comes down to one thing," remarked Mr Davis, "money."

There were clapping and shouts of approval at the manner in which Mr Davis had expressed himself, and at the speed with which he had come to the heart of the matter.

"And it is money I ask you to give this child, my friends, so that his future can be assured, to the extent of what you bestow on him."

One of Armstrong's friends stepped forward and placed a dollar note on the table. Others followed until a pile of notes and coins formed a little mountain beside the iced cake.

Armstrong was impressed by his father-in-law's eloquence. He had never got to know him well and regretted it. He spoke as Armstrong always dreamed of speaking. He was, in short, master of the word, of that powerful element which was in the beginning.

When Mrs Armstrong came forward with her husband to cut the cake, her eyes were moist.

One of the women remarked, "When I see two people happy like that it brings tears to my eyes."

The young people were anxious to get on with the dancing and while the table was being pushed back into the corner there were murmurs of approval from them. Two of them had had too much to drink and were sitting on the chairs against the wall, their heads bowed.

Alice had enjoyed the company of one young man, but did

not know what to do to attract him back to her, without endangering her reputation. She suddenly wished that her parents were not there so that for once she could act as she wished. The two shots of rum she had drunk, against the express strictures of her father, had brought a warmth to her whole body, a warmth she had never before experienced.

Over by the wall a girl was sitting on a young man's lap and the mere sight of such a commonplace scene filled her with the strangest desires. She went out on the porch and waited, for what she was unable to say; then a few minutes later she went downstairs and waited, but no one came and nothing happened, except that, when the music stopped someone started calling her name from the landing. It was her mother. She quickly turned and went back upstairs.

"What were you doing there?" her mother asked reproachfully.

"I was looking at the crotons," Alice said limply, feeling slightly sick at the effect of the alcohol.

People began to drift away at about midnight until, by two o'clock, only a few were talking in the drawing-room. The floor was strewn with cigarette ends trodden flat and pieces of paper and matches. The Davis family had departed before the musicians, and when Armstrong made a little joke about hearing a cock crow, those remaining took the hint and said goodbye.

Esther, who was sleeping in her mistress's bed with the baby at her side, had to be awakened to make something for the Armstrongs and to give the infant its final feed before morning.

Alone in the kitchen she took it into her head to play mothers with the infant and undid the buttons of the cast-off garment she wore as a nightdress. She placed his mouth against her small breast; but the offering gave him no satisfaction, and after a few vain and increasingly frenzied attempts to secure a grip on it he gave up in a fit of yelling. Esther then hurriedly took him up into her arms, while his milk bottle, newly filled from the thermos flask, cooled sufficiently to start feeding him.

4

Seaweed and Bitterness

As the months went by, Armstrong seemed to lose interest in the boy. He no longer romped with him on the floor or took him on his lap. To Gladys's remark about his neglect he objected that he found Boyie as engaging as ever, but that he was waiting until he was old enough to run about and play a game of cricket. He would buy a real bat for him and they would then play out in the street with his friends.

"That'll be the day," his wife remarked cynically.

Armstrong's father died a few months after the christening, and left his son his two cottages; but to his daughter he left his thriving wheelwright business.

Bitter at the inequitable distribution of the estate, Armstrong found little consolation in his promotion to Postmaster of a Georgetown post office. With his father's business he could have retired and lived as he had always dreamed. Of what use was the money to his sister, ugly and unmarried at thirty-two? How could his father, who treated her like a slave during his lifetime and never let her out of his sight, leave her a business about which she understood nothing?

Gladys took her sister-in-law's part. Armstrong's sister was alone and the business would give her something to occupy herself with. If her sister-in-law understood nothing about it, neither did her husband. Armstrong, blind with rage at her disloyalty, called her a "blasted cunt", but her only reaction was to look at him with mute satisfaction.

The following week Armstrong was sent away to help organise new post offices in various parts of the country, and it was only six months later that he came back to a home where he felt himself a stranger. However, his wife, whose bed had been cold for so long, welcomed him ardently. Gladys's changed attitude softened his manner towards her somewhat, but his feelings for her had cooled even before he had gone away, so

28

that now he began to look around for a mistress with whom he could spend the evening hours.

At times he and Gladys talked until late at night. She agreed that it was unjust that his sister should have come into the bulk of his father's inheritance. With the income from the business Boyie could be given a university education.

At odd moments when they were just sitting on the porch he would catch her looking at him intently and, flattered by her affection, he began courting her again. But at other times they sat and listened to the sounds at night, the bull-frogs croaking and the dogs barking, and watched the lights in the house opposite.

Once, when she heard him tapping his feet to a tune he was humming in a low voice, she believed that they had begun again from the beginning, after he first came to her house in Queenstown and was obsessed by her ankles. They were married despite her sisters and were embarking on a life-journey. She had longed for him when he was away, recalling the sweetness of copulation, which became for her the heart of their marriage, so that she visualised his return as the start of an endless coupling of ineffable satisfaction, in which her anxieties would dissolve like salt in a cup of tepid water.

In the middle of a conversation he would go over to her and kiss her on the cheek and then on her mouth, and while undoing her bodice he would gently pull her into the bedroom and on to the connubial bed where, amidst the bedclothes, he would rediscover the passion of their first days together.

When Gladys told her husband that she was expecting her third child his happiness was complete. In a burst of activity he had the roof reshingled and the house repainted, and hung two maidenhair ferns in baskets in the gallery. He informed his friends of the impending birth and began making plans for the child's education. He even visited his wife's family in town, whom he professed to dislike, to tell them the good news.

On leaving, he thanked his mother-in-law.

"Thanks for what?" she asked, taking him by the arm.

"Just thanks," he answered, feeling his chest swell with goodwill towards all his wife's family.

"What a funny chap!" his mother-in-law remarked to her husband when he had gone away.

"He's never got a crease in his trousers, you noticed?" Mr Davis observed.

"D'you think they're going to be happy?"

"Never can tell with these people," declared Mr Davis thoughtfully. "So many of them're getting jumped up these days. Types like him will be working in the Civil Service soon, mark my words."

"Well," put in his wife, "the better he gets on the better it'll be for Gladys. She hasn't got the grit the other two have. If things go wrong she mightn't be up to it."

The child was born a weakling and died in its third month. And for some strange reason Gladys Armstrong found herself weeping months after the infant's death, as if it had been her first-born. Armstrong, mystified, made vain efforts to console her, assuring her that she would have others who would grow up as healthy as Rohan and Genetha.

"I know," she said. "It's not that I don't know. . . . What it is I can't tell. The tears just come . . . by themselves."

However, the weeping stopped after the dead infant appeared to her in a dream and spoke like a wise old man. He was happy where he now was, but if his mother continued to weep as she did she would make him unhappy and afraid.

And after that Mrs Armstrong was wont to tell Esther and the neighbour who lived opposite that her dead child had only come visiting, as if that remark explained her grief and its vanishing.

Then in the following months a rift again appeared in the marriage. Armstrong invariably interrupted her attempts at conversation by reminding her that he was reading and had to give back the book by a certain day, or by watching her blankly and then asking, when she had finished, what it was she had been talking about.

In time they found little to say to each other and Armstrong became so irritable that Gladys got into the habit of speaking to him through Esther. On the slightest pretext he went out and often returned home in the early hours of the morning; and if she enquired where he had been he would reply that he was with friends who frequented a cake shop in Georgetown where they played draughts.

One Saturday night he took her for a carriage ride to the sea-wall on the edge of Georgetown. The children waved excitedly to their parents while the cab driver waited patiently, as listless as his horse; and after Gladys and her husband had climbed in, a flick of his whip was sufficient to start the animal trotting down the unlit road. The children were so carried away that Esther was obliged to restrain them lest they fell out of the window.

Gladys Armstrong's heart was pounding at the thought of the drive past the big sugar estate just outside Georgetown and the railway crossing at Lamaha Street. Perhaps they might come back by way of Camp Street where the tall tamarind tree was. Lower down, there were the black-pudding and souse stalls and the peanut sellers. They conjured up the time when she was free and went walking with her sisters and parents in Regent Street on Saturday nights, and she stole glances at the boys when under her father's watchful eye. More than once she fell head-over-heels in love with a young man she saw for the first time among the crowds in Regent Street, and swore she would marry no one else. A chance meeting would bring them together again at some time in the future and then she would introduce him to her parents. She would sit at her window every afternoon, scanning the faces of the young men who passed by, in the hope of catching sight of the object of her secret passion.

"I asked if the shaking of the carriage's worrying you," Armstrong enquired, annoyed that he had to repeat his question.

"No, I don't feel anything."

Satisfied that nothing was wrong he fell back into his silence.

They reached Upper Camp Street, where the absence of shops and the cool breeze contrasted with the hurly-burly of Camp Street and Regent Street. At last the carriage drew up alongside the band-stand and the couple got out. They climbed the flight of stairs leading to the embankment and took another flight of stairs down to the beach. The tide was far out and the sand glistened wanly in the moonlight as they stopped by a tuft of dead grass which rose out of the beach where it was overlaid by mud.

Suddenly Armstrong found himself struggling with a wave of irritability that seemed to have no cause. The presence of his wife, the strong wind, the noise of the surf, like the breathing of some leviathan, the money spent on the journey, everything seemed designed to put him out of sorts. She was walking beside him, stubbornly silent; yet, he knew that if she spoke her words would only contrive to deepen the sense of futility he felt. Why could he not accept things as they were, recognise the failure of their marriage and settle for a guarded peace? After all, it might be a good idea to permit her to go home to her parents from time to time. But he would never do that; it would only make things worse.

Her thighs were becoming thick and her breasts flabby. Yet whenever he thought of taking a mistress his conscience reproached him. It was damned absurd. Everybody did it and even boasted of it. Since his promotion and the acquisition of the two cottages there was no longer the excuse that he could not afford it.

Every time he broached the subject of his cottages and the difference the money was going to make to their lives she went into her shell, as if there was something unhealthy about their ownership. Why not divorce her? And start the whole business over again? The choosing of a partner was no different from being blindfolded and picking the first girl you touched. Besides, he would miss the children, and it was doubtful if he could keep the servant when they separated. There must be some way. . . . His weakness was showing such concern for their relationship. He needed only go on as if he were happy at the way things were. She would be the sufferer, since he went out and met people and saw his friends in the evening when he needed a game of draughts or a few schnapps of rum.

At this point in his reflections Gladys tripped over a stick camouflaged by a mass of seaweed, and involuntarily she held on to his arm for support. The slender thread of his composure snapped and, turning round, he walked briskly towards the sea-wall.

32

"Where're you going?" she called out.

"Home!" he replied brutally, leaving her standing, a solitary figure on the beach.

"Sonny!" she called to him by his fond name; but he kept on across the sand, then climbed the stairs and disappeared over the wall.

She was left alone on the beach, standing as if rooted to the spot. She looked out to sea and for the first time the idea of suicide came to her. It was said that the sea claimed at least seven victims a year, as of right, fishermen mostly, who robbed it inconsiderately. From Gladys's old home in Queenstown the incessant roaring of the waves at flood-tide could be heard at the dead of night, like a jaguar on the prowl. No one in her house spoke of it, in a tacit denial of its very existence, though the wall along the coast was proof of an obsession. The sea and those birds with curved beaks that hovered on the edge of her youthful dreams, limpid-eyed and expressionless. Then, after dwelling on the possibility of suicide for a while, she began to make her way to the sea-wall.

A couple were going by, arm in arm. She was slim and her skin was tight. The young woman's backside curved as Gladys's had before she had children. As she approached the couple she noticed that they were not in fact arm in arm; rather, the woman was holding the man's arm as if grappling for dear life, or out of fear that he might run away.

Armstrong sat waiting for her in the carriage; and when she appeared and opened the carriage door she saw him looking out of the window in the other direction.

The carriage drove off to the sound of the clop-clopping of the horse while someone on the sea-wall laughed aloud, as if mocking her. And the rolling of the carriage gave her bad feelings and her back no longer seemed to be supported by her spine, so that she closed her eyes in an attempt to forget where she was.

"What've I done?" she asked quietly.

"It's not I who'm sending you 'to your father's house', as you call it," he declared.

This was a reference to a remark she had made the day before when they had been quarelling.

"You know that even if I wanted to go home my father would drive me out," she observed.

"Home?" he shouted. "You still consider there home? When the hell are you going to wake up to the fact that you're married? Home!" he exclaimed scornfully. "You and your sisters went out once a week and you didn't know what went on in the rest of the world. I came from my father's house and my father's house was as good as your father's house. If I didn't talk about it, it's because I've grown up. You all cringed before your father and had to ask his permission even to open the window. The only difference between our fathers was that mine punished me with the belt while yours punished you by not talking to you for days. And you threaten me with going back to your father's house. . . ."

"I wasn't threatening you. I was just saying—"

"What's the kiss-me-ass difference?" he sneered.

She tried to say something else, but he uttered a sound of impatience which brooked no further talk. The carriage rolled along Main Street, under the flamboyant trees, the amber-tinted street lamps and past the mansions of the rich. The flamboyants were in bloom and the pedestrian walk that divided the two arms of the road resembled some covered garden where couples strolled hand in hand under the flowering trees. The rhythmic sound of the horse's hoofs on the pitch echoed down the side strets, giving Armstrong a reassurance he sought in his frustration.

"Probably it was not like that at all," he thought. "Maybe she loves me and talked of her father's house because I'm always in a bad mood. But if I was bad-tempered yesterday was she not the cause? Oh, God! If only I knew." The best thing to do was to allow her to go and see her people, to go home as she called it.

"Home!" he thought, roused to anger again. "But home is my house!"

The carriage went past La Penitence Market and crossed the bridge into the suburbs.

When they reached home, Armstrong's anger had abated. He helped his wife down from the carriage and paid off the cabbie; then the cab turned round ponderously and drove the fifty yards

34

home. Armstrong followed his wife up the stairs and thought, as he gripped the balustrade, that it was in need of repair.

5

The Servants

Esther had come to work for the Armstrongs when Mrs Armstrong was carrying Rohan. The arrival of the carriage in Little Diamond had caused a stir, except, as Esther remembered, to her own family who had been expecting the woman from Agricola the day before.

After much talking between her parents and the brown-skinned lady, she remembered leaving the hut and walking down the village street between her mother and younger sister, in the footsteps of Mrs Armstrong, who was lifting her dress slightly in order to protect it from the mud of the dirt road. And even then, at the beginning of their acquaintanceship, she was striving to copy Mrs Armstrong's walk, as later she was to imitate her speech and her gestures.

It was only months later, when recollections of Little Diamond came to her without her seeking them, that Esther consciously looked back at her childhood and youth, at her parents, her brothers and sisters and a house of endless births.

The night Esther's father went out in search of her eldest brother with her two maternal uncles was a landmark in her life. They found him drunk on the Public Road and brought him home. He was only sixteen, but responsible for organising the family's work in the fields. Her two uncles stripped him and held him down in the yard while her father flogged him with the cow-whip until blood came and the neighbour's wife shouted out in protest. The power of those men — in a village where there were women bringing up a family single-handed — the helplessness of her mother, revolted her. And from then on she dreamt of going away from the village, her hut and the cloying stench of asafoetida.

On learning of the woman's coming visit and her wish to have one of the girl children, Esther prayed that she would be chosen, in preference to her sister who was nine, three years younger than she.

In the carriage, while they were on their way to Agricola, Mrs Armstrong spoke to her for the first time.

"I'm expecting. Do you know what that means?"

"Yes, miss, You belly goin' get big," came the prompt reply.

"You must say," corrected Mrs Armstrong, " 'You are expecting a child'."

"I understand, miss," said Esther.

And those simple words contained the message of her inordinate ambition. Esther understood. And, like a sponge, her understanding sucked up all she saw and heard, all the things that separated her from the Armstrongs, the brass that had to be cleaned on Sundays, the daily dusting of furniture, leather-bound books, vast umbrellas, shoes, elegant lacquered boxes and the repose of flowers in vases with flaring tops.

There grew in Esther a fierce attachment for the Armstrong children. She took them to church, even after Mrs Armstrong no longer went, and was once entrusted with Genetha on a trip to Georgetown — Rohan was too young to accompany them — where they went to see the ocean-going ships rising above immense wharves, and the barnacles that clung to their hulls. Genetha marvelled at the ebb-tide and the driftwood from up-river, and at the shining bodies of the stevedores.

Back home Esther felt betrayed when Genetha ran and threw her arms round her mother.

"The neighbour said you were a capable girl, Esther," Mrs Armstrong remarked, pleased at the success of the outing.

"Thank you, mistress," replied Esther.

"I can't understand how you learn so fast. It's uncanny. Some people take weeks to learn to do a simple stitch; but you. . . . Are you happy?"

"Yes, mistress."

"Don't you miss your family?" pursued Mrs Armstrong, who lived in fear of Esther's mother taking her away when she discovered how accomplished she had become.

"I'm sure I do, mistress."

"You're sure you do?" enquired Mrs Armstrong, not knowing what to make of the girl's answer.

"Yes, mistress."

"Would you want to go away if your mother came for you?"

"I don't think so, mistress."

"You're not sure, then," remarked Mrs Armstrong, attempting to conceal the anxiety she felt.

"I am sure, mistress."

Mrs Armstrong smiled. The girl would never express herself with less equivocal words. She was like that. If she were a boy, people would say that he was destined to become a lawyer.

And this disinclination to give a direct answer exasperated Mrs Armstrong in the end. It was impossible to get near the girl. Should she ask her opinion about the meal for a particular day or enquire about a neighbour, Esther would answer so deferentially and give so little away that her words amounted to a prevarication. She resented this girl from Little Diamond, who was nevertheless indispensable to her way of life.

Mrs Armstrong gave up her attempts to get close to Esther, and the latter felt more at ease with a distance between them.

The arrival of Marion, the new servant, more than four years after Esther herself came to live with the Armstrongs, brought Esther close to panic, for the girl, a good year younger, would surely compete with her for the children's affection and her mistress's trust.

One night she dreamt that the Armstrongs went to Georgetown, taking the children and Marion, and left her behind to look after the house. She pretended not to mind, but secretly hated Marion for it. The next morning when she found she had only been dreaming she was all the more incensed.

The feeling of foreboding Marion's presence aroused in her dogged her for weeks and it was only grudgingly she showed the new girl how to set the table and do the hundred other chores of the household.

Esther often lay awake at night, mulling over her anxieties, when the silence was only broken by the barking of a dog. Beside her, on the floor, was Marion, her mouth open and breathing deeply, while a few feet away lay the two children, prostrate on their iron frame bed.

Yet, as time passed, Esther lost her mistrust of the younger servant and even came to regard her as a friend. One night when the family were out they decided to raid Mr Armstrong's rum bottle. It was Esther's idea. She knew where the rum was kept, under his bed. She poured out the cane spirit into two cups and made some lemonade, which she mixed with the rum in the cups, replacing the missing spirit with water from the goblet. The two girls were soon giddy and giggled long and senselessly, and went to the window from time to time to see if the family were coming back. Then Marion wanted to take some more rum, but Esther was afraid.

Emboldened by her euphoria, Marion showed her friend how they danced in Mocha. She writhed and wined violently, urging Esther to imitate her, but she could only flail her arms and throw her body around like someone who had never danced before. Marion laughed so much that tears came to her eyes. She held Esther by the waist and tried to demonstrate the rhythm by pushing her to the right and to the left, but to no avail. Esther pulled herself away and began to dance after her own fashion.

When, on going to the window, Marion saw the family coming up the street, the two girls rushed down the stairs and ran to the back of the yard, where they hid behind the latrine. No one called them and Esther suggested that they wash out their mouths with trench-water. Then they crept along the ground in the tall grass until they reached the trench. There they lay on their bellies and rinsed out their mouths with the brackish water.

Once, when Armstrong was not at home, Marion had a long conversation with her mistress.

"You're happy, Marion?" Mrs Armstrong asked her, putting the same question to her that she had asked Esther.

Mrs Armstrong, elegant in her mollee and simple frock, had large eyes set in a dark brown face.

"Yes, mistress."

"You miss Mocha?"

"Yes, mistress," she answered, intimidated by Mrs Armstrong's cordiality.

"Agricola is bigger than Mocha, though, and there's the police horse on Saturday night. Once one of the boys in the village pulled a hair from its tail. You can imagine the commotion. . . . You think I'm good-looking, girl?" she asked out of the blue.

Marion, open-mouthed, stared at her.

"Well, answer," Mrs Armstrong ordered. "Don't be afraid. Speak the truth."

"You nice, mistress. Even with you grey hair you nice."

Mrs Armstrong bit her lip and stared hard at the girl.

"Tell me something, Marion. Do you really like me?"

When she saw that the girl was once more thrown into a state of confusion she went on without waiting for an answer.

"I wasn't vain when I was young, but now I'm getting older I spend hours before the mirror. I cut a bit of hair off at the temple and wish I could put it back again. I've got some of my hair from when I was eighteen years. Wait, I'll show you."

She went to the chest-of-drawers, rummaged in it for a while and then took out a box covered with faded blue paper. Opening it carefully, she showed Marion the strands of jet black hair, neatly held in place by a thin length of wire tightly wound round it. The girl could only see it as hair with no significance except that it was a different colour from the hair Mrs Armstrong now had.

"You see . . . don't touch it! Just look," Mrs Armstrong urged.

She placed the wound hair against her own and went up to the mirror of her chest-of-drawers. With a brusque movement she put the memento back into the box, which she hastened to replace in the drawer.

"If only you could see people behind closed doors. . . . I don't know why I'm telling you all this. Promise not to repeat a word to Esther."

Marion shook her head.

"No, mistress."

"Do you like Esther?"

"Yes," Marion answered at once.

"The children like her," said Mrs Armstrong, "I don't know why. There's something disturbing about Esther. More than once I've caught her watching me as if she knew something. I don't know what there is to know. The hurtful thing is that she can run the house single-handed. She knows how to save money and how to spend it. When there's no money left it's then she cooks the things to make your mouth water. She picks callaloo in the back-dam and breadfruit from the church-yard. And then with bird-pepper and pigeon peas from the yard she does the rest. You see, I haven't anyone to talk to. . . . You know all of this already. Are you tired of listening?"

"No, mistress!" exclaimed Marion.

"You had a boy friend in Mocha?"

Marion bowed her head and said, "No," softly.

"Look out of the window and see what the noise is."

Marion went to the window. "It's a man selling something on a cart," she said.

"Doesn't matter; I haven't got any money."

There was a short silence.

"Esther doesn't talk much," Mrs Armstrong continued. "But she watches and stores up in her mind what she sees. Do you like people who see and pretend they don't see? But I'm a Christian so I'm bound to like Esther. Look, Esther talks to you. You're the only person she's taken to — no, it's true. She's taken to you. I can tell. You must come and tell me everything she says. Promise. Promise?" she asked eagerly.

Automatically Marion nodded.

"You're lucky, Marion. Everyone likes you. You're fresh and you laugh from here." And saying so Mrs Armstrong put her hand on her chest.

"When I was your age," she continued, "everyone used to say, 'She's nice-looking, she's beautiful,' and they would walk away, just as I wanted to say something."

Her voice faltered as if she had been hurt by a recollection.

"If only I lived in Georgetown," Mrs Armstrong went on, "I could at least sit by the window and watch the people go by."

There was a pause, painful for Marion, who attempted to get up.

"No, don't go yet. I'm dying to give you advice. But it would be useless in any case, because you wouldn't take it. And if you did you'd regret not having had your own way."

She paused again and looked at Marion fixedly.

41

"Marion, do you dream?" Mrs Armstrong asked, emphasising these words in a remarkable way.

"Sometimes, mistress."

"Do you ever have wild dreams about strange men crushing you and biting your face and beating you to the ground?"

Her eyes were staring; then catching sight of Marion's expression she added quickly, "I don't have that kind of dream, but one of my servants used to. She was before Esther's time, you understand. Go on with your work now," she ordered, looking at the girl from the corner of her eye.

Marion was to remember that conversation for a long time afterwards, as if she had engaged her mistress in a contest and had got the better of her. Some of the awe with which Mrs Armstrong had inspired the girl had disappeared, lost in that inexplicable influence of words. Mrs Armstrong must have felt the loss, for immediately after the conversation she treated Marion with unwonted harshness, while showing Esther a deference that surprised the older servant.

6

Season of Galoshes

In Agricola, Gladys Armstrong was regarded as being mad. People said she only wore black at home and fed the bats that hung from the eaves. It was her husband who drove her mad, they said, for he had nothing more to do with her.

Gossip also had it that she was afraid of her own small son. One of the servants had confided in the grocer that Mrs Armstrong would sometimes hold him and stare into his eyes and then push him away from her, saying, "Go away. You resemble your father too much."

Her guitar had aroused curiosity from the time she and Armstrong came to live in the village. She had bought the instrument as a substitute for the piano she could not have after she married.

"Who ever heard of a woman playing the guitar? I bet he drag she from Panama or somewhere like that. You only got to look at she face," one woman opined.

But it was only since Marion came and she was completely freed from the housework that anyone had heard her play. When on a warm night the sound of her playing drifted away into the darkness the neighbour with the cherry tree in his yard would say to his wife, "You hear that? She alone again. He tell she more than once he gwine tek it away if she play it. You wait!"

And the sound of the playing and the noise of the night insects would accompany one another.

She taught Marion a few chords on the instrument and the girl, in time, became a better performer than she was. When, once, she heard her playing for Esther a new calypso called "If you can't stand the digging, give me back me shilling" she took the guitar away and forbade her to play it for a week.

"I think Mr Armstrong's got a lot of money in the bank, Marion," Mrs Armstrong once said to the younger servant.

"You don' know?" Marion asked.

"He hides his bank book," replied Mrs Armstrong. "But he left a letter lying about telling him to send it in for the interest to be recorded. You know, I've only been to see his house once. He doesn't talk about them," Mrs Armstrong went on.

"He don't talk at all," Marion declared.

"He talks when he's with his friends. I know. . . . Can you smell something burning?"

"Is Esther," Marion reassured. "She make a fire in the yard with the grass that Baboo cut."

"He even gets the grass cut every month."

"I going go an' help Esther with the burning," Marion declared.

She was dying to tell Esther about Mr Armstrong's money in the bank.

"No, stay here with me."

"You should get a friend in the village," Marion suggested.

"The midwife used to come and see me; but somebody told her I said things about her that weren't true and she never came back. Me! Say things about her! Whom do I talk to? And who talks to me? I talk to myself half of the time."

"I know. I hear you."

"Well, don't tell anybody," Mrs Armstrong warned. "You know what they say about people who talk to themselves. What can I do if no one's there to talk to? In the night when you're all sleeping I listen to the radio and pretend it's all happening in the drawing-room. . . . I just had an idea."

"What?" Marion asked.

"I'll ask Mr Armstrong to buy a newspaper every day."

"You think he'll do it?"

"I think so."

"But I kian' read good enough to read a paper," Marion protested.

"Esther can read for you."

"I suppose so. But she in' going always be in the mood," Marion said.

"Nonsense! She'll like showing off."

Gladys Armstrong placed her hands between her head and

the back of the chair, leaned back against them and closed her eyes. Marion, thinking that she had fallen asleep, got up and tiptoed out of the room.

After she had gone Gladys opened her eyes and thought for a moment of going to fetch the children from school. She did not like them lingering in the road, and besides, the walk would do her good.

Why was Marion not as ambitious as Esther? She seemed content to speak as she did, to let others read for her. Her only goal appeared to be to get married and to bring children into the world. Was that really all there was to life for women? To breed children and obey their husbands? And there was little doubt that Marion would grow up to be more contented than Esther. Was little Genetha's life to be a repetition of her own? What would be her lot if she braved her father and married the man she loved? What would she do when he said, "Obey or get out"? Would she dare get out? Could she afford to?

The smell of burning grass and the sound of laughter rose from the yard and Gladys Armstrong sighed and began to get dressed.

Children were running along the road on the way home, while others were standing in knots in front of the school. A boy bolted out of the school yard into the street. It was Boyie, she thought; but when he turned round she recognised him as a boy living across the public road in Jonestown.

"I don't like you coming to meet me. I'm not a baby."

The voice came from behind her. Boyie had been speaking to a friend who lived opposite the school and on catching sight of his mother waiting for him he left the boy to come over and protest.

"I didn't come for you. I came for Genetha," she lied.

"Oh," he muttered, disappointed.

Instead of going back to his friend he began to kick the ground with the tip of his right shoe. A minute later Genetha appeared in the company of another girl who shyly smiled and walked away. Gladys and the children started off home when, suddenly, Boyie said that he did not want to go home right away.

"Why?" Genetha asked.

"Is none of your business," he said sharply.

"Don't forget to be home for tea," his mother reminded him.

He did not answer, but darted away.

"What did you do at school today?" she asked Genetha.

"Nothing."

"All day?"

"Well, a little of everything. I came second in spelling."

"Who beat you?" asked her mother.

"Mavis. She always guesses the right answers."

Mrs Armstrong smiled and remembered her own school days. Boyie never spoke about what went on in school. In fact, he resented being asked. If she tried to enquire from his teacher how he was getting on he would never forgive her. So she was left in the dark as to his progress.

"Mrs Strachan said she's going to lend me a book to take home and read," said Genetha, "and Joy said she could read better than me and she should have the book to take home. And Mrs Strachan said Joy was rude and she had a big head and was not the best in reading. I know she's the best in reading and I don't know why Mrs Strachan said she wasn't and Joy won't talk to me and she said she wasn't my friend any more and she wanted her skipping-rope back. And I said I didn't have her skipping-rope and that I'd given it back to her and she said that I wasn't to play with her any more."

All of this came tumbling out like the contents of a bag that was turned over in one movement.

"You like school?" Mrs Armstrong asked.

"Only when I come first," Genetha answered.

"Does Joy like school?"

"I don' know. She says she does, but she says one thing one day and something else another."

They continued to walk while Genetha skipped for a few yards and walked a few more.

"Is Boyie good at school work?"

"Don't know," replied Genetha.

46

Mrs Armstrong then asked her daughter if she wanted any sweets.

"Yes. A nut-cake."

On the way to the shop she skipped so much that Gladys let go of her and allowed her to skip ahead. She bought two nut-cakes for a cent each and kept one for Boyie.

"That's the bigger one you're keeping for Boyie," protested Genetha.

"No, it isn't. Now stop that," her mother reproached.

Genetha sulked for a while, but was soon herself again.

"Joy's mother buys her the nut-cakes for a penny."

"Some children never eat nut-cakes in their whole lives," Mrs Armstrong told her daughter.

"Is Joy's mother rich?" Genetha asked.

"I don't know," her mother replied.

"She must be," said Genetha after a moment's reflection, "to buy Joy nut-cakes for a penny. A whole penny!"

"A whole penny!" her mother mocked her.

That night Gladys Armstrong sat looking out into a street where no one passed by and nothing ever happened. It was ten o'clock by the ponderous grandfather-clock that stood on the floor against the partition. The street was unlit and the bushes by the paling and the gutter could barely be made out in the shadows. If she stayed up long enough she would see the cab driver come home. He would get down from his seat, unhitch the horse and lead it across the bridge and under his house. He would then reappear a few minutes later to lower the hood of the carriage. Then, lifting the two shafts he would pull the carriage over the bridge and under the house where it remained until morning. The routine was invariable, but it was something to look forward to. The sound of chains, the two lamps lighting up the street, the jaded horse standing mutely between the shafts, ensured a certain poetry. Sometimes Armstrong came home before the cabman, at other times after him. She had taken to rushing to bed and pretending to be asleep whenever she saw him coming, as she was unwilling to face him when he might be bad-tempered or drunk.

And so the months passed. The rainy season gave way to the

dry and the dry season to the floods of January. The bridge was under water and the children caught the red, plump shrimp that came in from the canal simply by placing two baskets across the gutter. Then, the night air was heavy with moisture and there was an infinite sadness about this season of raincoats and galoshes, about a cabman who never uttered a single word, and a grandfather clock that ticked away one's life with a reassuring sound, resembling nothing else on earth.

7

The Arrangement

Armstrong told his wife that there were rumours of the sugar market collapsing. The country depended on sugar, he told her, and God knew what would happen if they could not sell the year's crop.

The foreboding in the air about sugar's future was echoed by the newspapers. The *Daily Argosy* warned against the dangers of panic and when, the same day, it was announced over the radio that sugar sales on many foreign markets were suspended those who held sugar shares tried to sell them at whatever price they could get. There was talk of suicides and a rumour that there would be a budget deficit. Several sugar estates were in danger of closing down and the government had drawn up plans for retrenchment and suspended recruitment to the Civil Service.

Gladys followed the crisis in the newspaper her husband brought home every day now. The gloomy forecasts all seemed to be correct and the news, followed over the radio and in the newspapers, filled people with dismay. Prayers were said in the churches for the recovery of the economy, the poor state of which was attributed by many ministers of the church to the wickedness the people of the country had courted in a time of plenty.

One of these men of God, the Reverend McCormick, gave sermons that attracted considerable attention. They were dubbed by the newspapers "The Doom Sermons", for reasons evident in an extract from one of them:

"Like Sodom and Gomorrah you sow what you reap and like Sodom and Gomorrah your harvest will be destruction. When the fire falls from the sky and you can hear the sword being fashioned by the smith it will be too late, you generation of lechers. From this very pulpit I warned you time and time again, when you were fattening yourselves and your children, when you were wearing bright clothing and bedecking yourselves with jewellery; but you turned away like disobedient sheep. And now you come whining to me. This church has never been so full, not only with your sinful bodies, but with your fears. Look at you down there, your frightened faces gazing upwards as if I can help you. Only He can help you, provided you can rouse his compassion and trust. I tremble to think that you have fathered children, you who are incapable of guiding yourselves. You trust no one, not even your employers or your ministers. Take the strike that was called at the sugar estate last week: was it necessary? Haven't your employers looked after you like a father his children? Turn away, turn away from the path that led the Gadarene swine to their destruction and follow the way of the Lord."

The sermon was published in full by one newspaper, which also ran an editorial gleefully approving it and calling for an end to wage rises. The interests of employers and employees were identical, it said; if the one suffered so did the others.

One night, on returning home, Armstrong found Gladys entertaining his sister.

"Well, is what bring you to look me up?" he greeted her. "One thing I know, you didn't drop in on your way to the poor-house."

There was no reaction from the visitor, who avoided her brother's eyes. Gladys made a sign to him to desist.

Looking from the one to the other Armstrong waited for an explanation.

"She's got something to tell you," Gladys almost whispered as she got up from her chair and left the drawing-room.

"Ask Esther to light the other lamp and bring it," he called to Gladys as he went towards the kitchen.

"I know what you think of Father and me, Sonny. But you've got to help me!" his sister blurted out.

He stared at her, his face masking a feeling of satisfaction.

"I've lost a lot of money. I had twelve hundred dollars in sugar shares. . . . You know I don't know much about these things."

Armstrong's eyes opened wide.

"Twelve hundred dollars!" he exclaimed, his words followed

by a high-pitched whistle. "Where you get all that money?"

His sister put her hand to her mouth and coughed. She looked up and faced him, as if imploring him for something.

"Father left it for me," she answered reluctantly.

"With the business?" he asked.

"It was part of the cash that went with the business."

Armstrong got up from his seat, his hands thrust in his pockets. At that moment Esther appeared with the lamp, which she placed on the dining-table.

"Haven't I told you a hundred times not to put a lamp on that table?" Armstrong said irritably.

He took the lamp from her as she lifted it up from the table. After looking for a suitable place to put it, and finding none, he laid it on the floor near to his sister, so that it lit up her face in a grotesque fashion. His wife came back into the room.

"It sounds like a lot of money," his sister said, "but it only brought me in eight dollars a month. With the rent I get from a house I bought I could just make ends meet."

"And Father didn't even say a word to me about what he was leaving," observed Armstrong. "I always wondered why there wasn't any cash. But you were always sly. Even when he was dying, even then you made him believe he was going to live. Well, I couldn't stand his eau-de-cologne, his white kerchiefs and—"

"I know you had a hard time," she began.

"A hard time!" Armstrong exclaimed. "A hard time! He was always saying he'd be glad to see the back of me, yet if I wasn't in by a certain time he'd curse and shout."

Armstrong was almost frothing at the mouth with rage.

"Oh, Christ! I wonder why I did stick it so long," he went on. "Anyway he died like an animal. When his friends saw that he wasn't getting up any more they didn't bother to stick around. And those friends who took out his coffin took him out head first, not caring how he went. If he'd only seen how few people came to his funeral!"

He sat down, hardly able to contain his anger.

"But you," he continued after a while, "you played your part to the end. He and his kerchiefs."

"I did love Father," she said quietly, but defiantly. "And you don't have any right to talk about him like that."

Armstrong stood up again and looked down at his sister's frail figure; her expensive clothes annoyed him immeasurably.

Months ago he confided in a friend that he had forgotten about his family. His father was dead and there was no point in holding anything against him. He no longer held it against his sister for receiving the bulk of the inheritance. Now, as all the old hatreds that lay dormant in him were flaring up, he took in his sister's pointed shoes, her watch and shiny handbag. One more provocative word out of her and he would chase her out of his house.

Armstrong got up and began pacing up and down the room. He had not yet taken off his bicycle clips, which gripped the bottom of his trousers in such a way that, in normal circumstances, he would have appeared a figure of fun. Gladys was frightened and sorry for him, but she could not keep her eyes off his sister, whom she had imagined as a large imposing woman, a female version of Sonny Armstrong. Every time Armstrong spoke she seemed to shrink in her chair, like a nail in a hole, under the blows of a hammer.

If only Armstrong realised what a lonely woman his sister was, and that, with tactful handling, she would have been willing, on their father's death, to accede to any reasonable arrangement regarding the property that he might have suggested, his manner would have softened towards her. It was his stubbornness and his uncompromising attitude that had come between them, more than any selfishness on her part.

She had come to ask him to help her sell the wheelwright business at a good price. In the end, he said that he did not know if he was prepared to help, but that if he changed his mind he would come and see her.

Gladys accompanied her to the Public Road and saw her on a tram.

When Gladys returned home she found Armstrong sitting at the table. He had taken up the lamp from the floor and had put it in the middle of the table, precisely what he had forbidden the servant to do an hour ago. In his excitement he called her "Glad girl".

"What d'you think of that, eh, Glad girl? We'll see. We'll see. But you noticed how, though she came to beg, she still wore her fancy shoes? They come from New York, you know. You could see New York written all over them. Oh, yes! You got to hand it to her. She can dress."

When he was sixteen he used to stand in front of his sister's petticoat and stroke it and then, once he had looked round to make certain that no one was watching him, he would bend down and look under it. That petticoat folded over the clothes' horse had cost him many a sleepless night.

"Yes, she can dress," he repeated. "Now let's see: a thousand dollars, less advertising and lawyers' fees. That would make about nine hundred and fifty dollars. I could even buy the business from her myself."

He mused over the possibility of acquiring his sister's business, and as he flirted with the idea he began to think seriously of the obstacles in his way. It occurred to him that while he was at it he might suggest selling her house as well.

The very next day he made enquiries as to the money the business and property would fetch and he was advised to "Sell now!" The bottom would *soon* fall out of the property market as was happening with the other markets.

The very next day he went to see his sister and told her the bottom had already fallen out of the property market and that she would have to sell at once at a give-away price. He, however, anxious to become reconciled, would buy the property at a reasonable price she herself would fix. She agreed to sell for four hundred and fifty dollars and thanked him for the trouble he had taken, and for his generosity.

Three months later the Armstrongs moved into the Foreshaw Street property in Georgetown. The bottom-house room was reserved for his sister, to whom he let it below the price a similar room would fetch.

Gladys suspected what was going on, but dared not ask him. Besides, the dream of living in Georgetown again was realised when it seemed for certain that she would be buried in Agricola for the rest of her life. The fact that the house was in Foreshaw Street, not far from her parents' home, was of little importance. They were to live in Georgetown; and even if it had to be in a range-yard she would have been content.

8

The Move

Armstrong decided to move house at night. Like that he needed to hire no more than a dray-cart, for the darkness would effectively hide his possessions.

The children and Mrs Armstrong took the cab to town, while Armstrong himself accompanied the dray-cart and its driver. At first he tried to ride beside them, but found the pace so slow, he was forced to dismount and make the journey on foot, pushing his bicycle all the way.

A smoking kerosene lamp swung beneath the rickety cart, while Armstrong's own bicycle lamp cast a faint ray on the furniture, piled precariously behind the ass. The metal casing of the wheels made a grinding noise on the gravel and rattled over the bridges spanning the canals and trenches while, from time to time, a late vehicle went by in a cloud of dust.

On the outskirts of Georgetown, where the sugar-cane was in flower and all the frogs of the cane fields seemed to be croaking, Armstrong was anxious that his household goods, held in place by a deftly tied rope, should not fall off the cart. Occasionally he made the cartman stop, so that he could adjust a chair or retie the rope to ensure that it was firmly secured. This concern was greeted by a succession of suckteeths and glances of scorn from the cartman, who would not waste any words on his hirer and his wretched possessions.

A strike of municipal cleaners had just come to an end, but the men in their carts had not yet had time to clean up the vegetable peel and rotting fruit lying around the vast wrought-iron market place in Bourda. The stench in Orange Walk, over which the cart was now making its way, was overpowering, and even the cartman, accustomed to daily excursions to wharves and the incinerator, was obliged to press his nostrils together.

Then, a few hundred yards further on, all was clean in residential Queenstown, the unblemished district, with its tall houses and blossoms on year end, and painted palings like flattened spears embracing yards darkened by thick branches of fruit trees.

Gladys was waiting at the window of the empty house for her husband.

Armstrong wanted to take in a mattress first, so that the children could sleep on the floor; but Gladys thought that in the excitement they would be unable to fall asleep anyway, and so they remained up to wander round the house and watch the bedsteads, commodes and other heavy pieces moved in.

A group of children gathered round the cart and amid the clatter of kitchen utensils one of them shouted out, "Look the po!"

They all exploded in a volley of laughter at the sight of the enamel chamber-pot. Armstrong pretended to reach for a gun in his breast pocket and at this the group dispersed immediately, frightened and delighted at the same time. But they continued to watch from afar in little groups, approaching a bit closer as each piece of furniture came off the cart.

"Is what that t'ing, man?" one of the children asked. "You ever see a t'ing like that?"

This remark was prompted by the appearance of the ornamental pedestal.

"Is what that for, man? Fo' put the po 'pon?" the wit persisted.

The groups of children burst out laughing again.

"You stupid or what, man?" another boy asked. "You can't sit 'pon a po on top o' that thing. You want to shite you'self with fright?"

Another roar of laughter followed this, for by now the youngsters, who were again close to the cart, were prepared to laugh at anything.

"I bet they come all the way from the bush. I bet that furniture an' all full-full o' snake."

Armstrong, afraid of making a fool of himself, pretended he had not heard these observations.

"Them not bush people, man. Them is a special people they call 'po' people."

The laughter that followed this was almost unbearable and

Armstrong decided to go inside and remain there for a while. But the observations and laughter continued unabated. And when the commode appeared and its lid flew open, revealing the tell-tale hole, the hilarity became an uproar.

"Look at that thing wit' the hole in the middle. Is wha' you put in that hole, mister?" the wit asked the imperturbable cartman.

"You batty!" exclaimed another boy, pre-empting the cart-man.

Two women passing by could not resist chuckling.

"The po first, then you batty; else you might as well do it 'pon the floor."

"Look the racking-chair. Me gran'mother got a racking-chair," put in a very small boy who had until then not spoken.

"He grandmother got everything," a voice said scornfully.

"But I bet she in' got the t'ing with the hole in the middle, though."

"Shut you mouth!" the youngster spoke up boldly. "You never even been in me gran'mother house."

"You call that t'ing she living in a house? Is a fowl coop, man."

But before the boy could defend his grandmother, someone noticed the guitar, which the cartman was holding in his left hand, while in his right he held two upright chairs.

"Look that violin. I wonder which o' them does play the violin?"

"I bet is the man. When he sitting 'pon that high thing shitting in the po he does play the violin."

"That's what you call making loud music."

The other laughed but not as heartily as when Armstrong was there.

Someone shouted out in the direction of the house:

"Mister, come down quick, you furnitures falling to pieces."

But, unable to tempt Armstrong back out, the groups began to disperse, until only two barefoot boys of about four or five years old were left to see the rest of the possessions in.

Inside the house Gladys kept threatening the children with bed if they were not quiet. She was preoccupied with thoughts about the neighbours. Were they friendly? Did they have difficult children? Did they have dogs? Through the window she could see the well-lit street, the verandas of the houses opposite and the people who occasionally passed by on the road. Even the dingy cake shop they saw on the way seemed different from the shops in Agricola. It seemed to beckon you in.

Although much had not changed since she was married and went away, she felt like a stranger rather than someone who was coming back to the district in which she was born and spent her youth.

In the end all the furniture, utensils and boxes filled with goods were piled pell-mell in the drawing-room. Armstrong paid off the cartman, who disappeared round the corner in his empty cart, as slowly as he had come when it was full.

The night was damp, with rain threatening every moment, and only the odd passer-by could be seen hurrying home on foot or on his bicycle. A drizzle began to fall, noiselessly spattering the window-panes in fits. The children bedded down on the mattress, the iron members of the bed having been placed on the floor of the small bedroom, to be set up the following day.

And after the children and servants were asleep, the Armstrongs found themselves talking to each other. Gladys was sitting on a straight-backed chair, while Armstrong was squatting on a box, opposite her. The uncertainties that plague those who move into a new house and a new district had brought them together.

Armstrong looked straight at his wife, as in the old days, but she avoided his eyes.

"I used to go to that school, at the corner of Albert Street," she told him. "I think it's Albert Street. And the shop at the corner used to be owned by a man called Bertram. We used to buy shave-ice there on Saturday nights. There's a baker somewhere round the corner too. Funny how you forget things like that."

She kept avoiding his eyes, and he, noticing that she was trembling, went over to her. He kissed her on the mouth while stroking her breast with his right hand, and she whimpered like a puppy in pain. Armstrong lifted her off the chair on to the floor and bared her legs, pulling her drawers halfway down. Then, a few feet away from the sleeping children they made love on the floor, for the first time for three long months, so that she shuddered violently and hoped that he would not tire.

In the adjoining room Esther and Marion were lying near each other. Esther, who had not yet fallen asleep, reflected that she was the only one who saw the move as a change for the worse. While Marion was encouraging the children in their excited chatter during the drive to Georgetown, behaving like a "never-see-come-fo'-see", and Mrs Armstrong kept leaning forward to take in all the sights, restraining her own excitement under her dignified behaviour, Esther alone remained unmoved. After all, it was in the house in Agricola that she had started a new life and, like many people who look back on their first job with an inexplicable feeling of nostalgia, she held fast to the memories of those early days, like Boyie's birth and the discovery of books not meant for school.

Only a week ago she heard a school teacher, who had recently retired, talking to Mr Armstrong about the first class he had ever had.

"I can remember all the names on the register," he had said, "just as if it was today."

And he proceeded to reel off the names of the children in alphabetical order.

That was how Esther felt. And because she felt that way she was unable to understand the feelings of the children, of Marion and of Mrs Armstrong.

The drizzle had become a downpour under which the leaves of the trees in the back yard swished and sighed, and the rain pounded the shingle roof where the water poured into the gutters and into the large rain-water vat in the back yard.

When the rain stopped the street was asleep, while gusts of wind shook the trees, which gave up their water. The street lamp clattered in the wind, and above, the angry-looking clouds massed and fled, exposing for a brief minute a bright, full moon.

9

Dismissal

Marion and her mistress had become all but close friends and, unknown to Mr Armstrong or Esther, the servant was given a little allowance. The two women were often closeted for long periods, to the chagrin of Esther, who had to be satisfied with the children's affection as wages for her devotion.

"I hear Esther telling somebody she don't get pay," Marion told Mrs Armstrong one day. "And this person tell her she should make you pay her, 'cause all the servants in Georgetown does get pay. But don't tell her I tell you."

"The ungrateful girl. After all I've done for her," Mrs Armstrong rejoined. "Who was she talking to?"

"I don't know the woman," Marion replied.

"But you heard it yourself?"

"Yes. I hear it myself. But don't tell her I tell you," Marion urged anxiously.

"What did she say exactly?" Mrs Armstrong pressed her.

"She say a lot of things. She say you and Mr Armstrong don't hardly talk to one another. And she say you don't like her although she work her finger to the bone for you. I kian' remember all she say."

That same night Gladys asked Esther if she had been talking about what went on in the home, suspecting nothing of Marion's malice. Esther denied that she had. When asked whether she had told anyone that she was not paid, Esther admitted having been asked by the woman at the bakery if she was paid and telling her that she was not. It was not she who had brought up the subject. Mrs Armstrong made it plain that she did not believe her, but Esther insisted that she was not lying and said that she was prepared to face whoever gave her the information. However, Mrs Armstrong replied that that would not be necessary.

Afraid of the consequences of Marion learning that she had not kept her word, Gladys Armstrong wanted to tell Esther not to say anything to the younger servant; but she could not bring herself to ask her this favour and risk that haughty nod of the head that irritated her so much.

That night Gladys decided to tell her husband about Esther's conduct, but he came home gloomy and uncommunicative. She let him be and was glad when he went into the gallery, away from the rest of the household.

Following on rumours of dismissals — as part of the government retrenchment measures — Armstrong and a number of postmasters had received an official letter marked "O.H.M.S." that morning. With trembling hands he had opened his, to find that his salary had been reduced by a quarter. He nearly wept with relief. But as the hours passed his relief was replaced by resentment at the cuts that would have to be made in his spending. He had paid for his sister's property with money borrowed from the bank in anticipation of the sale of the Agricola home, which, however, realised much less than he expected. Consequently he was obliged to raise a mortgage on the Georgetown house in order to pay the difference. He was no better off than he had been in Agricola, what with the new mortgage and the considerably higher rates and taxes. Besides he was obliged to let the houses at a low rent, for gradually, as a result of the recession, boards advertising houses "To Let" had sprung up all over town.

Late that night when Gladys came out to bid him good night he told her of his salary cut.

"One of the servants will have to go," he said. "I just can't afford to feed so many mouths."

She was in favour of dismissing Esther, but Armstrong thought that Marion should leave as she had been with them a shorter time and was the less responsible of the two.

"What you got against Esther?" he asked her. "She worships the ground your children walk on."

"That's one side," replied Mrs Armstrong. "I can't trust her."

And in answer he made a gesture of impatience.

"Just because she doesn't like listening to your endless complaints!"

Armstrong's remark had struck home.

"Marion listens to me, yes. After all, I don't have anybody to talk to."

Armstrong, touched by the confession of what he had known all along, capitulated. Esther would go.

"Only, don't tell her when I'm at home," he said to his wife.

And the next day Gladys Armstrong told Esther that her husband said that he could not afford to keep her.

"You can always come and visit the children whenever you want," she added, in a sudden access of sympathy for the young woman.

Esther had suspected that something was in the air. Since she had been questioned about what had happened in the bakery she could not suppress a feeling of uneasiness. But the sudden blow left her speechless and she kept looking at Mrs Armstrong as if the older woman had struck her.

"It's not the end of the world," Gladys Armstrong remarked, unable to find suitable words of reassurance.

"Where'm I to go?"

"Why, to Little Diamond, back to your people," advised Mrs Armstrong.

"What am I going to do in Diamond? You came for me and took me away — but I can't go back. You took me away and now you're sending me back. . . ."

Mrs Armstrong, disarmed by Esther's helplessness, was tempted to change her mind; but her fear of offending Marion was enough to make her stick to her decision.

"I'm sorry, Esther."

"Marion won't take care of the children, you'll see," Esther warned.

Gladys Armstrong did not reply and Esther stood there, looking at her as if there were another solution which depended only on her. Then, irked by the servant's unwillingness to take no for an answer, she said:

"Haven't I given you everything I've given my children? Didn't you read whatever I was reading and put on what I wore? Compare yourself with any other girl in your position. Compare the way you talk now and the way you used to talk. My God! You even talk better than Mr Armstrong."

"I'm only a servant and can't do anything else," observed Esther.

"I'll give you a testimonial; and the way you talk you won't find any difficulty in finding a job in one of the big houses."

A wave of desolation overcame the young woman. The day after they moved to the new house Mrs Armstrong sent her back to Agricola to look for some brass, which was missing when the things were unpacked. When Esther stood in the drawing-room of the empty house, surrounded by space where once were chairs and lamps, brackets, a pedestal, window blinds and all the bric-à-brac that go to make a house's soul, she closed her eyes and listened to the silence. There she had become a woman, shedding the garments of her girlhood in the corner of the bedroom, alone and untutored. She remembered how she had lain on the floor, afraid that something terrible had happened to her; she was being punished for some wrong she had forgotten. She prayed that the fault in her body would be healed and wished desperately to confide in Mrs Armstrong. But she found her own solutions and later discovered that Nature had not dealt with her in a singular fashion.

A cup still lay on the kitchen dresser, where it had been left by Marion, who had been responsible for collecting up the crockery. The vat tap was dripping; it was she herself who had neglected to switch it off properly. In the morning heat a number of marabuntas were circling languidly under the mango tree, heavy with unpicked orange-coloured fruit. She sat down on the lowest step of the back stairs. On the paling which divided the yard from the neighbour's a lizard was scurrying, pursued by another, each appearing and disappearing in turn behind the staves until they went out of sight for good, hidden by the concrete pillar of the empty house. Had they really left this place for ever? She heard a child's voice coming from the direction of the Decembers' house across the trench. . . .

On the way back to town she was unable to get the house out of her mind. She would return, she thought to herself, and then remembered that the next time someone else would be living there. The furniture would be different and the blinds would be a different colour, and the sounds issuing from it would be different.

"Can I stay here until I find another place?" Esther asked Mrs Armstroig.

"Of course, Esther. As long as you like."

That night, when everyone else was asleep, Esther sat at the window looking on to the back yard. In the dark she could see nothing except the outlines of the houses. She went out front and sat by a casement window, through which shone the garish light from the street lamp. In town the people seemed tight-lipped, unfriendly and intimidating, she mused. Then her thoughts turned to Marion. From the first moment she set eyes on her she knew that the younger girl would contrive her fall. Never before nor since had she had such a presentiment. . . . Where would she work? In a mansion or in a cottage like the Armstrongs'? How was she to start looking for work? Ought she to go from house to house? She knew no one in town, unlike Marion, who had already made friends with a young woman who worked for a lawyer in New Garden Street. She was also on speaking terms with the grocer, who gave her credit without demanding to see her mistress. She got the best pigtails from him and free salt; and he even introduced her to his wife, saying how nice the servant was. Esther detested Marion from the bottom of her heart.

"They'll see how much she cares about the children!" she found herself saying aloud, as if she were speaking to someone in the yard.

After Esther had gone, Gladys Armstrong experienced bitter pangs of regret. The young woman had been with the family for eleven years and had left her imprint on their way of life. Boyie adored her. She used to read him stories from the newspapers and magazines and feed his taste for fantasy with talk of Masacurraman, Old Higue and other lore figures. She loved him as if he were her own, and believed that his rebelliousness was not unnatural, but something to be appeased, a form of energy to be transformed into something constructive. When he made a sling-shot to shoot birds she showed him how to trap them with bird lime, and then took the sling-shot away.

Mrs Armstrong had admired her way with her son and had wished that she would never get married before Boyie was off their hands.

It was impossible to tell if she missed Esther because of their long association or on account of her fears for the effect of her absence on Boyie.

10

Confessions

Since the move to Georgetown, Armstrong's estrangement from his wife seemed to take a decisive turn. He even neglected to observe the formalities of polite conversation he had maintained for the children's benefit. And in proportion to the couple's drawing apart from each other, the friendship between Gladys Armstrong and Marion developed, so that she became more a companion than a servant. She began to have a hand in spending the household money Armstrong gave Gladys; and when Genetha misbehaved she would slap her in her mother's presence; and Gladys, afraid of offending Marion, would say, "Do as Marion says, darling."

Sometimes, when Marion came back from market Mrs Armstrong found that she had bought ground provisions to make a breakfast different from the one she had planned. Once the servant came home with a string of crabs, which Gladys detested; but when she objected Marion sharply reminded her that she could not always please herself.

At other times Marion played the servant perfectly. She would massage Gladys's shoulders with soft, firm strokes of her fingers, till she groaned with pleasure. They would disclose to each other their innermost thoughts, as if their friendship was reinforced by the very difference in their social positions.

"Mr Armstrong hasn't been with me for over a year," Gladys once confessed. "Sometimes I get terrible headaches, but the doctor says it's because I don't get sufficient exercise. I know what it is, but I still go to the doctor. Over the past year I've taken more medicine than over the rest of my whole life."

One morning, just after Armstrong had gone to work, Genetha did something wrong and refused to apologise to Marion.

"I'm not apologising."

"Why?" asked Marion.

"I'm not telling you."

"You better!" Marion threatened.

"No!"

Marion raised her hand, but Genetha stared at her without flinching.

"Go on, hit me! I dare you to hit me. I'm not Mother, I don't care."

"You li'l bastard!" shouted Marion. "You watch! You going end up a street woman. You goin' see where them fine airs going get you."

From behind the door Gladys was listening, more embarrassed than hurt; and by the afternoon she and Marion were as thick as ever.

"I had a dream last night," Gladys told her during one of their lengthy conversations, "about Boyie. I was calling him by his right name, Rohan. He kept ignoring me whenever I asked him anything. I was getting all worked up, but I tried to control myself. Then all of a sudden he turned to me and said, 'Father doesn't like you any more.' I don't know what got into me, but I kept seeing little lights in front of me and it was as if I was floating, above and away, over the houses, away from Boyie and his father and everything."

Gladys's eyes were glazed, as if she had got up suddenly in the middle of the night and did not realise where she was.

"What happen then?" asked Marion.

But Mrs Armstrong did not reply to the question.

"It's Esther," she said vaguely. "I'm sure she'll do something to Boyie."

"But she gone," Marion said.

"My mother used to say," pursued Mrs Armstrong, "that some people pray for you and then something is bound to happen to you. They go to church and kneel down in a pew and pray and pray and pray until they know the prayer'll be answered. You can pray for somebody to get well, but you can also pray for them to get sick and waste away slowly and then die. And you know how Esther likes going to church."

"You got her on your mind," Marion remarked. "Tobesides, a dream in' got nothing to do with praying for you. If you ask me, Boyie not going to come to no good. I mean, they kian' even handle him in school. Look at the marks on his backside. Every day he get more and he don't care."

"I don't know, but I've never dreamt so much in my life as since I've come to live here. I'm always dreaming of Agricola, and yet I couldn't stand it there. The other night I dreamt of the cab man."

"Oh, him!" Marion said scornfully at the thought of the scruffy cab-driver. "What you dream then?"

"I'm not sure," Mrs Armstrong replied. "Everything was so confusing. I can't remember."

"Sometimes you frighten me the way you talk," Marion said.

"Don't you dream?" Gladys asked.

"Sometimes," replied Marion. "But not like that. In Agricola . . . you not goin' laugh if I tell you?"

"No," Gladys promised.

"Well, in Agricola I used to dream of the minister."

"Who? The young one?" Gladys asked.

"Yes."

"And what you dreamt about him?"

"You going to laugh," Marion protested.

"No, I promise," Gladys said, impatient to hear what her servant had dreamt of the personable minister of the village church.

"Well, I dream that one day he chase me down the yard and I fall under the jamoon tree. He then fall 'pon me — and it happen."

"What?"

"You know," Marion said with a giggle.

"What? In daylight?"

"Yes. What's the difference?"

"A dream's a dream," observed Gladys.

"Well, it wasn't exactly a dream," Marion ventured.

"You mean it really happened?"

"Yes. But not with him."

Gladys put her face near to Marion's and whispered.

"With who, then?"

"With the man next door. He was coming from he field and he give me two banana. He poke his finger in my stomach and say I was getting fat. Then he pretend to chase me and I begin to run. And when he did ketch me he put his hand round my waist and burst out laughing. I start to feel all funny inside. . . ."

"Here?" Gladys suggested, pointing to the pit of her own stomach.

"Yes, there," Marion agreed. "But really all over. And then he begin chasing me again and when he ketch me he did throw me down in the grass and ask me what I got in here."

She pointed to her bodice.

"And I say to him, 'Why you don't look?' And he laugh and put his hand in my bodice and start talking to me. And he say he going to cover my face with my dress, and he lift it up and cover my face . . . and then it happen."

Gladys felt strangely excited and wanted to be alone. Marion, thinking that she disapproved of her story, said, "If you want me to stop."

"No," replied Gladys.

Marion looked down at the floor, waiting to see if Gladys was willing to pursue the conversation.

"When I was a girl I never went out alone," Gladys said after a while.

"In Mocha," Marion said in turn, "the boys were always hanging round you, you know."

"I don't know, Marion. We used to watch the boys from the window and think about them, that's all."

"Well, as I say, in Mocha the boys was always hanging round you. But the one I did like never take hold of me and never ask me for anything, like the neighbour."

"Did it happen again? With the neighbour?" Gladys enquired.

"The next day I go to the house, when his wife out. He ask me what I did want, as if he never see me before. He so vex he tell me to get out of the house. 'You want to get me in trouble?' he shout. 'If me wife see you here she going kill me.' And when I stay by the door he fly at me and tell me to go away or he'd call the police. After that he never talk to me again."

Gladys looked back on the days in Agricola and tried to recall the neighbour and to connect him with Marion. He had a pinched face and his breath always smelt of alcohol. Suddenly Marion disgusted her. She was getting too full of herself. Her mother had always said you had to keep servants at arm's length, otherwise they became too familiar.

"We're going to the gardens today?" Marion asked.

"No, you've got the brass to do," Gladys said bluntly.

She intended to stop the rot, keep the girl in her place. Gladys Armstrong stood by her resolution for a few days, no longer helping her with the cooking nor accompanying her to the market in the morning, and if ever she ate alone she left the things on the table to be cleared by Marion. She even got her husband to speak to her about the way she swept the house, and when the young woman protested to Gladys about Armstrong's treatment she spoke to her sharply, reminding her that Mr Armstrong was her employer.

But with the passing days Gladys's loneliness overcame her pride and, as suddenly as she had rejected Marion's companionship, just as suddenly she took her to her bosom again, showering her with kindness. Gladys asked Marion to forgive her, while Marion denied that she had suffered any cruelty at Gladys's or her husband's hands.

And Gladys, as proof of her gratitude to Marion, made a confession she had been on the point of making more than once.

"People look at you and say, 'How you're lucky! See what you've got! You talk so nice!' And they fail to understand how pathetic and vulnerable you are. . . . I dread meeting people I used to know, because I've forgotten how to make conversation and would only make a fool of myself. And just the thought. . . . . I need my husband more than ever, but he spurns me as if I'm a leper. Yet in the old days when he came courting he was circumspect and kind and kept this side of him hidden from me. How people change! And now I've come back to live near my family it's too late because we hardly know one another any more."

Mrs Armstrong covered her eyes with her forearm, in the way young children attempt to hide from adults, without even turning their heads — a gesture that cut Marion's heart more than tears could.

At a loss for words Marion was about to say the first thing

70

that came into her head when Mrs Armstrong spoke once more, her head slightly bowed and her right hand still over her eyes.

"I protected him from my family, quarrelled with my sister on account of him. Could I do any less? He's the father of my children. For more than a year he hasn't caressed me and I've lost all confidence in myself. After Boyie was born he wouldn't touch me, as if having a child was a crime. I waited and waited, but he offered no explanation, not even after I said I needed him to sleep by me. I begged him, practically went on my knees and told him I'd do *anything* he wanted, provided he lay by me. God is my witness I was driven to it. It isn't as if I think of nothing else but that. Then when— Then he started taking an interest in me again and the third child came along. But it died soon afterwards, before it could be christened, before it had a name. Its tiny body withered and died, its tiny hands and feet and its tiny head withered and died. Mr Armstrong took the coffin under his arm and laid it in the hearse where it was lost among the white flowers and taken to St Sidwell's cemetery. And for weeks afterwards I would start crying, in the street, at table, on going to bed, and for no reason . . . as if all my children had died. . . ."

"My little brother and sister," broke in Marion, "dead before they was a year old too. And my aunt child—"

"You don't understand, Marion," Mrs Armstrong said gently, turning to face her. "Above all I cried because I knew that the child's death meant the end between Mr Armstrong and myself. He went further and further away from me, like a flock of dark birds. Throughout the world there are women who abort their children, millions of tiny aborted bodies are flushed away every year, some of them whimpering and screaming. . . . How innocent you are! But, you see, Nature does it without wincing. . . . I've never been able to understand my husband's bitterness. In my family we accept things as they are. Anyway, one day we'll all have to account before our maker for our deeds and our thoughts. Oh, yes! And our deeds. Do you know why I got rid of Esther?"

"No."

"She was in love with Mr Armstrong," Gladys went on.

"He did know?" asked Marion.

"I don't know. But I couldn't bear it. Since she came to live in Agricola with her girlish body, without breasts, she was in love with my husband. All these years I suffered the mortification of watching her love for him grow. Now you see why she was never interested in men?"

Then Mrs Armstrong fell silent, foundering in the exposure of her pain. She waved to Marion, who then left the room. And she shook her head, recalling her courting days and the days before, when she and her sisters would walk on the beach in a line, like country women, and edge round the little lakes of grey water that dotted the sand where the tide had washed the beach a few hours ago.

BOOK 2

Our furtive conversations
Were like lightning at evening
But your prints in the wet leaves
Where you stood
And your ringless fingers
Are all that I remember now.

11

The Epileptic Whore

Armstrong reduced his wife's allowance when his own salary was cut. Boyie's shoes were taken away from him when he came home from school in order to spare them, while Genetha's dress had to last all week. Gladys herself wore clothes at home that she would have cast off and given to the servant while they were in Agricola. The butter, which previously had been kept on the table and used at will, was now carefully rationed. Even Marion's white headdress, insignia of her status as servant, was not replaced when it began to suffer from constant laundering, so that the last evidence of rank that distinguished her from her employer was removed.

Armstrong was the only one to dress as well and eat as well as he had always done. He could not walk into his post office looking like a pork-knocker, he declared; and it was in the interest of the whole family that he should be well fed. In these days, when there were six men breathing down your neck, ready to step into your shoes when you went down with ague, it was no good saving on food. Look at Stuart, one of the best postmasters in Demerara. After four months on sick pay they retired him on a pension that could not feed an estate mule, and appointed a new man to Providence Post Office.

Yet, he could not ignore the dark rings under his wife's eyes.

"You should go to sleep earlier, like in Agricola," he advised her. "You used to go to sleep early there. Mind you, who can sleep through the night with all these stray dogs roaming the street and keeping up that racket. You pay your rates and taxes to run a city pound that doesn't even do its job."

"I sleep longer than you," she retorted. "In fact I spend half my life in bed."

Armstrong, despite his preoccupation with money matters, was happier that he had ever been. If in Agricola he sometimes came home at ten or eleven at night, he now did so regularly; and on Fridays he invariably crossed his bridge at midnight, tottering uncertainly as he put away his bicycle under the house.

He and his friends frequented a cake shop in a Kitty back street. After work, he used to ride the two miles or thereabouts from his post office in Lombard Street to see a school teacher friend who lived a stone's throw from the cake shop. At Doc's home another friend called for them and the three went off to play dominoes and drink beer until the shop closed.

On Saturday nights the friends were in the habit of going "on the binge", as they liked to say. Occasionally they walked to the red-light district in and around Water Street, where they drank with the whores.

On these excursions Armstrong at first felt like an adventurer in uncharted country; but in time, when he got to know the girls' names and developed a predilection for the smoke and liquor-scented rooms and the sound of the strident music, he looked on these sorties into depravity as outings into some forbidden but beautiful well of sin.

Sonny Armstrong was particularly taken by a whore named Lesney. While his two friends talked to the people round them he liked watching Lesney dance, mesmerised by the way she threw out her right foot. She danced with little effort, in comparison with the others; and her limbs, frail and supple, suggested a vague promise of repose. No one else seemed to share his high opinion of her good looks and, in fact, Doc thought her plain. Armstrong was afraid to dance with her, lest he made a fool of himself, so he confined his attentions to speaking to her. But her reticence made him so nervous he found himself taking twice as many pulls on his cigarette as he normally did, and, no sooner had he finished one than he lit another, a practice he abhorred in others.

Their conversations went like this:

"Thank God it's stopped raining," he would say. "Want a cigarette?"

She would then show him the cigarette she was smoking. After tapping with his fingers on the table and pulling up his socks, which were well secured by suspenders, he would then move his shoulders to the music.

"Want to dance?" he would ask.

76

Then, as she got up he would say, "We better wait for a slow piece. I like slow pieces."

At that point someone might come up to her and invite her to dance, thus saving him from further torture.

One Saturday night, inflamed by the skin exposed by her deeply-cut dress, he invited her to dance, throwing caution to the winds. He held her close, so that he could feel her small, firm bubbies against his body.

"Your place far from here?" he asked, emboldened by the effect of the rum he had drunk.

"Robb Street," she answered laconically.

"What about leaving now?"

"If you want to," she agreed, snuffing out her cigarette on the floor.

Armstrong bade his friends goodbye and left with the girl. She had put on a thin jumper against the cool night air. Once outside he was tongue-tied and they walked silently along the wet pavement, glistening from a recent downpour. He made up his mind to put his arm round her waist when they got to the next street lamp, and then, in full glare of the electric light he thrust his hand under her jumper and round her waist.

On reaching the building where she had a room she pushed the door open. Armstrong followed her along the corridor and up the stairs. On the landing she rummaged in her handbag for a key.

Inside the room she took off her jumper, then her shoes, before she sat down on the bed, her hands on her lap.

Armstrong went and stood by the window, from where he surveyed the meagre furnishings in the room, the chest-of-drawers on which stood a basin with a jug rising from its deep recess, painted with a floral design. A clean white towel hung over the lip of the jug and rested for part of its length on the chest-of-drawers.

Armstrong's eyes wandered towards the girl's naked feet, the toes of which were warped into the shape of the shoes she wore.

He turned to look out of the window. Below it lay the yard of a Chinese restaurant, over which was stretched a line strung up with dozens of thin-skinned, pink sausages. Vague outlines of kitchen workers seen through the back window of the restaurant were moving about like puppets behind a translucent screen.

Armstrong pretended to be interested in what he could see through the window, while in reality he was wondering how he should set about seducing the girl.

"It's her business. She does it for money," he kept telling himself. But whenever he turned round to look at her, at her dress, her unshod feet, he took fright at his intentions and clung to his post at the window. The shadows behind the restaurant window came and went at irregular intervals, providing a kind of accompanying suspense to his indecision.

Armstrong found himself looking through the window as well as at it, for imprinted on the glass was Lesney's reflection, immobile, slightly hunched. He saw her turn for a moment, no doubt to see what he was up to, only to turn back again to face the door. Then he saw her light a cigarette and exhale a horizontal column of smoke, which gathered in an irregular mass before rising slowly above her head.

"You don't ever talk?" Armstrong asked, joining Lesney on the bed.

"Yes."

"Why you so shy?"

"I not shy," she replied.

"You like dancing, eh?"

"Yes."

"What else you like?" he enquired in an attempt to get the conversation going.

But her only answer was to shrug her shoulders and then to reach out for the packet of cigarettes which she had placed on the wash stand.

"You like me?" Armstrong went on.

"You all right," she answered.

Hell, he thought, *I can't just throw myself on her like an animal.*

"You're comfortable?" he asked.

"Yes."

"You like me?"

"I say yes," she replied impatiently.

If it were not for her little bubbies, Armstrong would have

got up and gone home. He sat down beside her on the bed and drew her towards him, frail and unresisting. Her hair was parted down the middle and the two plaits joined in an upward sweep.

"You're so frail!" he whispered.

But she gave no answer.

He then opened her blouse, exposing her chest, and felt a strong urge to smother her in kisses. He felt her heart hardly beating and the apparent indifference only served to fire his passion.

"Open my trousers, ne?" Armstrong told her, while guiding her hand.

But, instead of responding, she slipped out of his arms and fell to the floor. He watched the contortions of her attractive face as the convulsions of an epileptic fit began to shake her whole body.

In an attempt to flee Armstrong opened the door, not understanding at first what had come over her. But at the head of the stairs he turned round and noticed a light under the door of the room adjoining the girl's. He knocked softly on the strange door and a gruff voice called out, "Is who?"

"Me," Armstrong answered.

"Me who?"

He knocked again without answering and waited until a middle-aged woman opened.

"Is who?" she asked pugnaciously.

"A girl in the next room. . . . I brought her home. She's got fits."

"Oh, Lesney," said the woman, her harsh expression vanishing with the words.

Turning round, she addressed an unseen companion.

"Is Lesney," she said, "she got a attack."

Brushing past Armstrong she hurried into Lesney's room. Then almost immediately she reappeared and went back into her own room, from which she emerged once more with a spoon in her hand.

"Gi'e me the pillow on the bed," she ordered Armstrong without looking at him.

Armstrong complied and the woman placed the pillow under

79

Lesney's head. Then, with Armstrong standing above her she watched Lesney through a succession of fits.

Some time later there was a knock on the wall.

"Stay with she; if I don't go now—" began the woman. But before she could finish a voice bellowed through the partition.

"How long you gwine keep me waiting, ne?"

The woman departed without more, leaving Armstrong to stay with Lesney who was lying flat on her back, legs apart and arms stretched out, away from her body. In between periods of calm her legs and arms would retract and then fly out violently and her head shift from side to side with each spasmodic movement. And Armstrong knelt by her, dreading an unexpected intrusion. Then the attacks ceased altogether and he was conscious of an unearthly silence round him and wondered how the young woman could stand it in that house on her own.

Before going away he placed a dollar note on the piece of furniture that passed for a dressing-table and went out into the night. His handkerchief was wet with the sweat he had wiped from the young woman's forehead.

When he got home he turned on the light in the dining-room, and noticing that the door of the kitchen where Marion slept was ajar, he went in and found her sprawled in the middle of the floor, her naked thighs exposed from turning in her sleep. Armstrong threw himself on her and satisfied his thwarted passion, while Marion made no effort to resist him.

The next night Armstrong sought out the prostitute again, partly because he could not get her out of his mind and partly to see if she had recovered. He took her back to her room, this time avoiding the well-lit streets.

"You're sure you're all right now?" he asked her.

"Yes."

He was put out by her inability to make small-talk; and to keep the conversation going he was soon telling her of his past and his dead parents.

He knew where his umbilical cord was buried, in the yard of the house where he was born. The tree that was planted over it must be quite large now, he told her. But Lesney was born in Georgetown and had never met anyone who set any store by that sort of thing. Nor did his disclosure that his father used to exercise with dumb-bells interest her either. But when he mentioned his mother she seemed to pay attention.

"A man used to come home every Thursday night to talk to her about controlling her life," Armstrong told Lesney. "And he taught her how to let her spirit leave her body and wander about the village."

"You believe in that?" Lesney asked.

"I don't, but she did. There are things you can't account for . . . like why I can't keep my eyes off you."

Then he began to speak of how he came to be attracted to Queenstown and everything connected with it, even the men who went round the well-maintained alleyways with cisterns of oil which they sprayed on the gutter-water to kill the larvae of mosquitoes that carried malaria.

"Something did draw me to those houses in Queenstown," he continued. "In the village I come from, with pigs rooting for food in the mud, lived a woman from town. I used to read the Bible to her because she had cataracts on her eyes and couldn't read for herself. Whenever she invited me into her house I used to tremble with excitement. Everything there was from a different world — the furniture, the window blinds, the lamps, the bed — everything. Her house was always quiet and sometimes my own voice frightened me when I was reading. At times I used to go up the back stairs and slip through the open door, but her ears were sharp and she almost always heard. 'Is it you, Armstrong?' she used to say. She never once called me by my first name. My wife talks like her and, even though she does everything I say, has got the same superior manner, as if you could never hurt her. . . . At times I wish for something to happen so that I can show my wife how much I care for her, that everything I do is because of this unutterable love. And yet I treat her worse than a dog sometimes. If I did tell you the things I did and especially the things I'd like to do to her, the humiliation I'd like to heap on her. . . ."

Then, with unexpected violence he remarked:

"I don't know why her family does give themselves such airs! None of my people even went to a card-cutter by night to find out if they'd ever get married."

Lesney, whose interest in what Armstrong was saying had

waned, asked: "You mean you wife sister been to one of them women to find out if she going get married?"

"Yes."

"I didn't know people like you ever do things like that," the prostitute remarked.

"Ha!" Armstrong exclaimed bitterly. "They do it secretly, at the dead of night. They only go up the back stairs; and when they reach home they prostrate themselves on a bed and inhale smelling-salts."

Armstrong waited for the young woman to pursue the questioning, but she remained silent. Then he began talking again, harping on his inadequate background, his in-laws' aloofness and matters that cut deep into his heart. He talked late into the night, of the isolation in marriage that breeds unhappiness, and of the guilt he felt on account of the lack of contact with his children.

"What you thinking about?" he asked Lesney unexpectedly.

She answered without hesitation. "I thinking 'bout how much you going pay me."

Armstrong, annoyed at the girl's lack of sensitivity, fell silent. Through the open window came the muffled sound of footfalls on the pavement and the occasional noise of horses' hoofs as a late cab rolled by. He recalled the night he took Gladys out for a carriage ride and his unkindness when she seemed receptive to his efforts at reconciliation. The wounds they had inflicted on each other were now beyond healing. What he had told Lesney seemed now untrue: he no longer loved her. And this knowledge came to him like a thunderbolt and with it a sense of relief, as if a knot in his heart had loosened.

Armstrong got up, rummaged in his pocket and took out a couple of bank notes, which he handed the girl.

"You not doing it?" she asked, a little surprised.

"No."

"Please you'self. Is because o' yesterday?" she enquired, with a sudden show of concern.

"The fits? No! I'll come another time, you'll see," he assured her.

Once on the pavement he walked briskly away from the house in the direction of his home.

12

Friends

The next day, a Sunday, Gladys Armstrong, the children and
Marion went to church and joined with the congregation in
celebrating Harvest and the reaping that comes as the reward
of man's labour.

On the following evening Armstrong went to look up his
school-teacher friend, after he had made sure that everything
at the post office was in order.

Doc was about forty and lived alone. His skill at dominoes
and card games had earned him the name "Doc" among his
cronies. Dark, with fine striking features, he was critical about
everything and everyone around him. Anyone who caught the
two men in conversation would have marvelled at the way
Armstrong listened to his friend's interminable monologues,
with that patience that springs from affection or great admira-
tion.

Armstrong, out of pride, had carefully concealed from his
friend the true state of his marriage. Doc, on the other hand,
seemed to take pleasure in recounting his failures.

"I want to talk to you before B.A. comes," Armstrong told
him. B.A. was their other friend.

"You're not in trouble?"

"No, no, it's not trouble," Armstrong replied.

The two men sat down, but immediately Armstrong got up.
He then told his friend about what had happened after he
left him on the night of Lesney's attack. He modified the story
here and there, neglecting, for instance, to say that he had
wanted to run away and leave the girl. Doc listened intently,
thinking that the story had an exciting end. Armstrong confessed that he was afraid of the consequences of the incident,
but did not tell of his return to the prostitute's room.

"But what could happen?" Doc asked. "You think that
because the girl had a fit you'll end up in prison? My father
used to have his bouts regularly, and when he fell down in

the house and started frothing at the mouth no one took the slightest notice of him. He'd be twitching on the floor and we'd be passing up and down like at the railway station. Sometimes they used to last half an hour. Man,,if|that's all you've got to worry about you're on easy street."

Then, drawing his chair closer and casting a glance sideways as if someone might be listening, he began to tell a story Armstrong had heard a number of times.

"Ha! You talk about trouble! When my wife and I were engaged she promised me milk and honey and everything you can think of. Anyway, that's neither here nor there. The point is you're happy. I'm not. I was after a headship some time ago; and some fellow whispered into the ear of a natural superior that I was an immoral man, because I'm separated from my wife. I mean, you're allowed to be an immoral headmaster, have your women on the side, drown yourself in liquor; but as a headmaster, not as an aspirant to a headship. Why I separated, eh? I separated because my mother-in-law was always in my house. Now, any self-respecting man would've shown her the door, and that would've been that. But where the women're concerned I'm no self-respecting man. I've never been at ease with them. It's not that I'm afraid, mind you; you might call it anxiety. With men it's different. I'm never at a loss for words, but when there're women about my tongue grows fat and I start grinning without knowing why. My legs start turning to water and my nose needs blowing; and every action you can perform with your hands I perform. Man, it's so stupid! Whenever my wife said to me she was expecting someone, I always wanted to run out of the house quick, before the lady even got to the gate. But I was no coward. Oh, no! I used to stand my ground. I mean, it was my house and my wife and my time. I used to go into the back room and practise: 'Howdye do,' I'd say. That was a mistake to begin with, saying howdye do to a woman. Anyway I'd say to the mirror, 'Howdyedo? Do come in!' And I used to work myself up into a state welcoming this woman. Oh, yes, I used to stand my ground and wait for her. But as soon as the bridge creaked I'd go lame.

"Anyway, as I was saying, my mother-in-law took it into her head to start coming to look after the baby. She changed it, cleaned it up, put it to bed and so on. She saved my wife a lot of work. But she was a pest, a menace on two feet. That woman intimidated me so much I was glad to get out in the mornings to school so I could push the children about and take it out on them. Especially the little girls who looked as if they would grow up to resemble my mother-in-law. The children used to call me the 'Hangman'. But it came to the point where I couldn't stick it any longer and I asked for a transfer to a Georgetown school. But they could only get me one in Truly Island. It was far enough and one Saturday I strolled down to Suddie Stelling as if I was going down to the sea for a walk. That was that. Freedom and eternal peace. And five years later I got my transfer to Georgetown."

"And what about the child?" Armstrong asked.

"What about my wife? What about my mother-in-law? God rest her pestilential soul!"

"You're not frightened somebody'll meet you?" asked Armstrong.

"I used to be," admitted Doc. "But you can't stay frightened all the time. Yes, man, you're lucky. . . . Sometimes I wonder if I did the right thing when I beat it. I hate the school I'm in. The teachers are afraid of the headmaster, who's afraid of the inspector, who probably pees himself when he's talking to the Director of Education. One day—"

Just then there was a whistle outside. Doc peered through the window and saw B.A. riding down the street.

"B.A.," he called out. But his friend did not hear him.

"He must've been whistling some time and we didn't hear him," Armstrong said, peeved that he might be missing his game of dominoes.

"Let's go down to the cake shop, ne?" Armstrong suggested.

"No!" Doc said, rejecting the idea. "He'll come back when he sees we aren't there. Then we'll all go down to the shop and play."

He went inside and came back with a big bottle of rum, already broached, but almost full. He had lit a cigarette, which was gripped firmly between his lips as he tried to pull the cork from the bottle. Armstrong helped himself to the rum, pouring the amber liquid into the glass his friend had brought him.

"As I was saying," pursued Doc. "'One day the headmaster asked me to take a letter to the Director of Education himself. Man! When I got there even the gravel in the drive was out of this world. The front door was open and I went in. The hall alone at the foot of the staircase was twice the size of this room. It was painted white and carpeted, and at the top of it was a climbing plant. As I went upstairs I could hear someone playing the piano; not your little tinkle-tinkle, bang-bang. No, the genuine sound like you hear over the radio at night, when the street is silent and it's the hour for listening. Oh, man, my skin did begin to crawl at that surge of music, and I thought to myself that of a sudden all the petty things in the world were blown away."

His face was transfigured as he relived the experience.

"Man," he continued, "I don't know anything about music. I can't tell anybody's major from his minor; but in all that sumptuousness, with that climbing plant and the scent of flowers from the garden, the new paint, that piano sounded rich and arresting. When I got to the top of the staircase I saw a man playing the piano, a big grand-piano, on which two men could lie down full length. He saw me and stopped playing. And then you know what he did? You know what he said? What Mr Bain-Gray said to me?"

His face was twisted in anger and he looked at Armstrong as if the latter had abused him.

"What'd he say?" Armstrong asked, eager to hear the story's end.

"He looked at me and in his educated, cultured voice, he said, 'Are you the new gardener?' You ever felt like spitting in someone's face? And yet, and yet this is probably the worst of it. When I said I wasn't the gardener and showed him the letter he said he was sorry, in his suave, persuasive voice; and I then regretted that I had felt like spitting at him. I told myself that I was too suspicious and violent. But whenever I look back on that visit I squirm, because I was right to feel as I did at first."

"Why?" asked Armstrong.

"While he wrote the note he wanted me to take back he didn't even ask me to sit down. There were chairs all over the place, straight-backed chairs, easy chairs, wicker chairs, enough for a whole regiment. But I stood among those chairs and waited. What's a chair for, eh? For sitting on? For leaning on? To rest your feet on? To copulate?"

His voice was becoming shriller and shriller, and at this point he got up and thrust his hands in his pockets, a gloomy expression on his face.

Armstrong could not understand his friend's excitement. A show of obsequiousness in the presence of his superiors was as natural as expanding and contracting his chest. Besides, from the story Doc told this Bain-Gray man was a pleasant fellow. But there was no crossing his friend when he was like this. In order not to commit himself he leaned forward and poured some rum into his glass.

Doc sat down again, took his cigarette from the ash tray, but did not put it into his mouth. A long cylinder of ash was about to break off and fall to the floor.

Armstrong felt uncomfortable, for he wanted to talk about Lesney. This always happened with Doc. You'd start out by telling him your troubles and just when you were getting into things he would recount a period of his life or an incident that bore no relation to what you were saying.

"The function of conversation," he once said, "is not to exchange views, but to relieve yourself."

The trouble was, he seemed to be continually relieving himself instead of giving his companion a chance.

A whistle from outside broke his train of thought. Armstrong looked out of the window and saw B.A. dismounting from his cycle. Doc called him up.

B.A. was indignant that Armstrong and Doc had let him go down to the cake shop without telling him that they were there. But a couple of shots of rum appeased him and in a short time he was shrugging his shoulders to no purpose, a sure sign that he was relaxed and felt at home. This curious tic had got worse since he lost his job as a book-keeper a few months back.

"In America they eating out of dustbins," B.A. said. "I tell you I prefer to be in this old country than America, 'cause you'll never starve. You can always go down by the dam and pick a mango or catch a few cuirass and eat them."

"But who want to eat cuirass?" Armstrong objected, revolted at the idea of consuming the notorious shit-eating skin-fish.

"You don't eat cuirass 'cause you still got a steady job!" B.A. rejoined hotly. "I talking 'bout people that in' got a job."

"In any case," Doc butted in, "in America there're employment benefits."

B.A. laughed scornfully.

"I wonder when they draw these benefits? Before they rummage in the dustbins or after?"

This remark annoyed Doc. Armstrong wanted to listen to the radio, so as to ensure that the evening would end peacefully, but Doc wanted to talk.

In spite of B.A.'s thin skin, his two friends missed him when he was not there. They missed his poor logic, his obsessive concern with neatness and above all the fact that he never complained. Armstrong's money troubles did not seem serious when B.A. was around, neither did the indignities Doc suffered at the hands of his headmaster. In fact, it was only in his sour presence that they could laugh often and heartily. But lately Doc and Armstrong noticed that a change had come over him. Where before he had smiled occasionally, now he seemed incapable of any display of mirth.

The three friends left soon afterwards for the cake shop in Kitty. But while playing dominoes a particularly violent argument broke out, during which Doc tactlessly made a remark about B.A.'s immaturity.

"Jesus!" exclaimed B.A., "look who talking! You think that by talking you can find a substitute for something. You're the biggest coward in the country," B.A. flung at him.

The shop-keeper was sleeping like a child, his body heaped in his rickety chair under the overhead bulb, which bathed his head and shoulders in a pale light.

Doc, stung by B.A.'s malicious remark, looked at him long and silently.

"Come, let's play," suggested Armstrong, making a show of shuffling the dominoes.

"You two make me sick," B.A. said in a voice throbbing with violence.

Doc lit a cigarette ostentatiously, inhaled deeply and then

exhaled a great deal of smoke, while Armstrong looked from the one to the other, desperately hoping that some unforseen remark, some unlikely occurrence would save the situation.

"What's eating you, B.A.?" Armstrong asked.

"So it's my fault, eh? Jesus in heaven!" B.A. exclaimed, at the end of his patience.

"I didn't say was your fault, but lately you're flying off the handle for nothing," Armstrong said in a conciliatory tone.

"I can't talk to people like you," declared B.A. "You hear the man insult me and you tell me I'm flying off the handle. All right, I flying off the handle, but I don't got to stay here with the two of you," B.A. retorted.

Doc and Armstrong listened to him crossing the shop bridge. Stunned by his behaviour they sat without knowing what to say to each other. It was Armstrong who spoke first.

"It's this damn trouble he's having with his son. If I was in his place I'd tell him to go and find somewhere else to live."

"You're sure that's what's eating him?" Doc asked.

"There's been talk."

Doc slowly replaced the dominoes in their box. B.A. seemed to have something against him, he reflected, for Armstrong always came off more lightly than he did whenever he attacked them. What if he stayed away for good? No, that was impossible.

"Let's go to Water Street," suggested Armstrong.

"On a weekday?" Doc asked, surprised at the suggestion.

"Why not? The girls're there every day."

"I don't have money for drinks. It's near month-end," Doc said.

"I'll pay," Armstrong offered.

Then, as they were leaving the shop he added, "He does worship his wife's memory," referring to B.A.

"The woman's dead and gone a long time; what sort of nonsense is that?" Doc said irritably.

When they got to Doc's house he went upstairs for his bicycle, which he hoisted on his shoulders and brought down the high staircase into the yard, damp from the continuous drizzle. They then rode to Armstrong's house where he went in for his raincoat. The two friends then rode off in the direc-

90

tion of Water Street to the whore-house they frequented on Saturday nights.

13

Jealousy

Since B.A.'s quarrel with Doc and himself, Armstrong resorted to spending more time at home. On Wednesdays he and Doc met at the latter's house to drink and talk, while Saturday was their night out in Water Street, where they had become regular clients. But the rest of the week found him stranded, as it were and sometimes, the mere sight of his house drove him to turn round and go to a rum shop before he returned home from work.

The first experience in Marion's arms had excited him, but with time he found her less and less desirable, knowing that everything she had to offer was his for the asking.

It was one day, months later, that he chanced to see her talking earnestly to a young man in front of the house. And from then on the young man and she met every night at the corner, under the street lamp.

One night when Armstrong went into the children's bedroom — where she sometimes slept — and attempted to caress her she repulsed him. The times when she had returned his embrace came back to him as he listened to her soft breathing. He recalled the surging of her body, and her even breathing now offended him.

Getting up slowly he left the room, not quite able to comprehend the finality of Marion's rebuff.

Marion was very circumspect, but this unwonted respect only riled him all the more; and deciding that it would be best to ignore her, for two days he feigned complete indifference. He addressed her in an off-hand way and when he settled in a chair by the window he would suddenly change his mind and go out for a walk instead.

On the second day, back from a walk he had not wanted to take Armstrong met Marion and her young man chatting at the gate. He stormed into the house and slammed the front door after him.

"The slut!" he exclaimed, half-aloud.

His wife came from the kitchen at that moment.

"What did you say?" she asked him.

"Nothing. I was talking to myself."

"Why did you come back so quickly?"

He gave her a murderous look. When he was alone again an irresistible force drew him to the shuttered window, which he flung open with such force that it rebounded into place with a clatter. Armstrong went to the door, opened it and closed it again, then he went back to the window and looked through the blind at the couple. Unable to restrain himself any longer he shouted out at the servant:

"Marion! Come in here!"

Marion addressed a few more words to her young man and then came upstairs.

"Where d'you think you are? In the back-dam in the country or something? You stand outside my house with a man friend as if you own the place. You're a servant in my house, remember that. And you'll damn well behave like one."

The children, who were playing under the house, crept up the back stairs and listened from the kitchen, while the mother and son who lived next door listened eagerly, having taken up a position at an open window without bothering to conceal themselves.

"Who's this man anyway?" Armstrong asked.

"Just a friend, Mr Armstrong," Marion answered.

"But who the devil is he?"

"Is the carpenter that working for Mr Dean."

"Well, let me tell you something. If I find you gallivanting with every Tom, Dick and Harry you meet you'll be back in Mocha in no time."

When it was all over the children ran downstairs, giggling and nudging each other. That same day Armstrong had abused one of the telegram boys for copying a message incorrectly, but when the youngster failed to defend himself he was overcome with regret and later gave him four cents. And that evening he was to be beset by a similar feeling for the way he shouted at Marion, mingled with shame at the way he had exposed his jealousy of her.

Gladys Armstrong, who had listened to her husband from

the bedroom, reflected that now everybody in the neighbour-
hood would suspect what his relationship with Marion was. On
first making the discovery some time ago she felt so humiliated
she believed herself incapable of living any longer; but with
time she accepted it as she accepted everything else. What else
could she do, she thought, when she relied entirely on her husband for support. She listened to Marion's confidences as before, but she herself could no longer confide in her, nor hold
any lengthy conversation with her. Whenever the girl caught
her looking at her they were both embarrassed, but pretended
that nothing was amiss.

She turned to Armstrong's sister for consolation and received
it in good measure. What did Gladys expect? It was a man's
world. Women were not in a position to change it and were
therefore obliged to accept it. The two women began to spend
a lot of time together, Gladys preferring to go downstairs to
her sister-in-law's room than to have her upstairs, an arrangement that her sister-in-law approved of, as she wanted to do
nothing that might offend her brother.

Armstrong's sister found a malicious pleasure in consoling
Gladys. She resented her dependence on her brother and had
come to feel that his motives in helping her to sell the business
some years ago had not been as altruistic as he had then pretended. She watched the progressive decline in the family's
living standards with satisfaction, taking note of the loose
paling-staves, the condition of the children's clothes and the
departure of Esther.

Gladys, for her part, envied her her friends, who visited her
regularly and at whose houses she often slept. It was they who
had awakened her to the possibility that her brother might
have swindled her.

As time went by she found it impossible to confine her resentment to her brother. She even came to dislike the children,
and more especially Boyie, whose boisterousness appalled her.
If her parents had been alive they would be sickened at the
behaviour of their grand-children.

Armstrong began to follow Marion greedily with his eyes. He no
longer went for walks at night, nor did he turn back at the gate

94

to go to the rum shop for a quick schnapp. Now that he was no longer able to have her, Marion's tantalising gait seemed even more provocative, as did the manner in which she combed her hair, while she sat in front of the looking-glass dressed only in her petticoat.

He invented excuses to send her to the shops, found fault with her dusting and the way she washed the shirts. All this Marion bore without a word of protest, until the night Armstrong's wife told him that the young woman wanted to be paid a wage.

"What?" Armstrong said, not believing his ears.

"She says that the other servants in Georgetown get paid."

"To think she had nothing when she did come to us! Where's she now?" he asked.

"Somewhere at the back of the house," Gladys said. "I'll go and get her; you'll only wake Boyie."

She came back a few moments later with Marion.

"Mistress told me you want money for your work," he said angrily.

"Is my sweetheart tell me that all the servants in town get pay," Marion spoke up boldly.

There was a certain insolence in her voice that aroused Armstrong, as if she were challenging him to refuse her request for a wage.

"You know you're ungrateful, eh? We bring you up in Georgetown and everything . . . but I suppose you're right. I'll make it fifty cents a month, but if you're not satisfied it's back to the village."

Gladys could hardly believe her ears, for she thought her husband would stand his ground. Marion went back to the kitchen, disappointed that she had not got a dollar, but willing to stay on for what was offered her.

That Saturday, when Mrs Armstrong and the two children went for a stroll on the sea-wall Armstrong, who was cutting firewood under the house, came upstairs, a pile of wood on his arm. He heard the shower and noticed the open bathroom door through which, under the streaming water, Marion was rubbing herself. She saw Armstrong stop at the open door, but made no effort to close it. He put the pile of wood down on the floor, stretched out his hand and turned off the water. Then, taking the towel, which was hanging on a nail, he started to wipe down his servant, gently at first and then more briskly, until he was embracing her and smothering her with kisses.

Armstrong was the happiest of men. At the end of the month he paid Marion her wage as he had promised and, in a fit of generosity, bought his wife a new pair of shoes. The children were given a cent each to spend and at their bed-time Armstrong told them a long story and made extravagant promises about the future.

14

From the Beginning of the World

It was a Sunday morning and Gladys Armstrong lay awake in
her bed beside her husband, who was still asleep. The house
was unusually quiet. From the widow's cottage next door the
sound of hymn singing could be heard, accompanied by occasional hammering from under her house. Marion ought to be
up, she thought, but there was no noise from the kitchen, nor
from the yard nor the children's bedroom. She could tell it
was going to be a sunny day from the keskidee calls and the
quality of the light.

Gladys was beset by a nameless unease. Her husband had
not increased her house allowance for a long time and to make
ends meet she had taken to using salt instead of tooth-powder
and to cutting down to the bare minimum the food she herself
ate.

Yet, something else was bothering her. She got up and went
into the kitchen, but Marion was not there. The young woman
was taking liberties, sleeping at that hour of the morning, she
thought. But Marion was not in the bedroom either and the
bedclothes on which she slept had been carefully piled in a
corner. Puzzling over the girl's absence she went back into the
kitchen and lit the coal-pot.

It was when she took down the pan from the dresser that she
found the note, which read: "My swetheart aks me to come
and live with him. I love him. Say goodbye to Boyie for me.
Tell Genetha I going give her the mony I say I giving her."

Mrs Armstrong went and sat down on the top of the back
stairs, the note in her hand. She had been a fool to be cold to
the girl after she found out about her and Armstrong. What did
it matter? After all, Marion was taking nothing away from her.

She had never confided in anyone as she had in Marion.
The nights they sat by the window talking and laughing and
making remarks about the men that went by! Sometimes they
counted the drunkards that passed the house, after the rum-

shops had closed, and speculated about what went on in these dens that reeked of liquor, out of which shouting and laughter came like belching from the belly of a contented diner. Were there any untoward goings-on? Did they ever talk about women? Marion did not think that they talked about women as much as women discussed men. Women did not play dominoes or cards or billiards or decide to go for a walk on the spur of the moment.

Gladys had often come near to telling the girl other things. When she was married she felt ashamed and inadequate, as if there had been some important lack in her upbringing. Had Marion stayed they would no doubt have become reconciled as they always had. Armstrong's sister could never share her secret life. Besides, how could she tell her things that would be, at the same time, a confession of her cerebral infidelity? Her sympathies would be with her brother, who neglected her and gave her only just enough money to live on.

"You know, sometimes I feel like giving myself to the ugliest man that passed by," she once said to Marion. "I mean I could choose the ugliest from the first twenty and invite him into the house and cook for him and then allow him to do with me whatever he wanted."

Marion had looked at her in astonishment, unable by any stretch of the imagination to share her mistress's feelings.

"I like good-looking boys," Marion rejoined, "with a moustache and a Buddy Jackson haircut. I couldn't stand a ugly man."

"I'd like him to hurt me," Gladys went on, as if Marion had not spoken, "as much as I could stand; and then, afterwards, punish me by going away without even thanking me. . . . Sometimes I believe I'm sick. Nobody's got these funny things coursing through them."

"You right. People don't think like that," Marion had said.

"One Christmas," she had told Marion on another occasion, "when I was about sixteen, my best school friend was staying with us; she drank too much of something . . . I can't remember what. Anyway, I liked this girl a lot and wanted her to come and live with us. She wore expensive clothes and talked about her aunt in the States and I admired her so much it was almost

98

painful. Anyway, she wanted to throw up after drinking a lot of something or other. As she leaned out of the window I begged her to vomit over my hand. And in the end it came out. When I was washing my hands under the kitchen tap I was glad and thought I'd never forget that day as long as I lived."

Marion was watching her, an expression of disgust on her face.

"You shouldn't talk like that after eating black pudding and souse, you know," Marion told her.

One day Mrs Armstrong confessed that she had dreamt she did not like her children. Then, after a moment's reflection she said, "How can I care about my children when my husband doesn't care for me?"

"You love Boyie, though," observed Marion. "You kian' hide it."

"Boyie'll marry some long-suffering woman who thinks it's her mission in life to be his carpet. The more he maltreats her the more she'll love him."

"They in' got many of them women round nowadays," Marion observed.

"You don't know anything about life, girl," Mrs Armstrong remarked absently.

"No man goin' take advantage of me, I can tell you," Marion said defiantly.

Now Marion had gone and she was left alone. In her parents' home everything had seemed so easy. The women obeyed and loved; the man dispensed security and affection. Had she married the wrong man or was there a deeper reason for the failure of her marriage? Her father used to say that happiness in the home depended on the woman, but she had given everything there was to give, forgiven when there was no need to forgive. Was her father wrong? Had he and her mother been really happy? But this was manifest. At night they took walks, arm in arm, down Vlissingen Road, made observations on the changes in the district and climbed the stairs with that leisure that spells contentment.

Gladys got up and re-lit the fire that had gone out and set about preparing the morning meal; but the smell of the toast made her feel sick. She leaned against the wall on her raised arms and began to cry bitterly as the rays of the sun filled the room. Next door somebody began to play a mouth-organ softly, but the tune glistened only briefly, then vanished like the ruby she once sold in haste. Gladys could not stop herself, even when she heard stirring in the bedroom and knew that one of the children had got up.

"Is what wrong, Mother?" Boyie asked, as he appeared in the doorway rubbing his eyes.

"Nothing. I don't feel well, that's all."

"Why not take some of Father's medicine?"

"I'll be all right."

"You burned the toast," he observed.

She took the hot, blackened bread and threw it on the table. "I'm hungry."

"I'm going to be ready in a minute, Boyie. Why not go inside and lie down again?"

"I'm hungry," he repeated.

"All right."

The Sunday unfolded as if nothing had happened. The kes-kidees gave out their shrill calls, the ice-cart passed at ten o'clock, the church bells rang and fell silent when the faithful were all gathered in; and there was discretion in the air. The hours were long and heavy, the hot afternoon following the hot morning and the warm night growing soft with shadows.

Gladys went to church for the first time since Esther had gone away, putting on the black dress she had had made seven years ago and leaving the house when the bells began to ring.

She sat at the back of the church and waited, like the others, for the verger to distribute the hymn books. The solemnity of the occasion brought back to her the passion she once had for church going, when in her early teens. And with that came fleeting memories of her passion for her husband — which used to flare up at the slightest manifestation of interest on his part. They came and went like those glimpses of colour in running water that vanish the moment they are perceived. But stronger were the recollections of communal singing and the mysterious power of the verger, with his long black coat, his deep stoop and fervent eyes.

100

Looking at those round her she had the impression that she was only part of a vast whole, that her own spirit had flown away, leaving her stranded with urges from another time. As a child she would — often without success — make a great effort to suppress her desire to show off, especially when a male came visiting. In some odd way she had lapsed into that childhood state, a prey to urges that came from deep within her, too deep for her to exercise over them the rigorous control she had been taught was necessary. Marion had provided her with the opportunity to behave absurdly at times, and so made it easier to accept the mask she wore in the presence of others. Now that Marion had gone she was continually haunted by the possibility of a loss of control. And yet, more powerful than the desire to escape death, deeper than the longing for happiness, was the longing to be herself, but in being herself to lose nothing; to wear the clothes of her choice, make friends with anyone who happened to be passing, and thereby discover her own true desires, her own morality.

Gladys had no idea why she had to come to church, like someone who walks along a once familiar path only to realise that it had been taken without any apparent reason.

"You're going to church? Why?" Armstrong had enquired. And there she stood, lost for an answer.

When the congregation rose to its feet Gladys rose with them. Having missed the announcement of the hymn she had to wait until the organ began playing the opening bars of the tune, which she recognised at once; and with just enough time to find the page in the thick, hard-bound hymn-book, she began singing with those around her:

> "Thou shepherd of Zion and mine,
> The joy and desire of my heart,
> For closer communion I pine,
> I long to reside where thou art.
> The pastures I languish to find
> Where all who their shepherd obey
> And feed on thy bosom reclined
> Are screened from the heat of the day."

Neither Zion nor Babylon had any meaning for her now; yet on hearing the start of the second verse, "'Tis there I would always abide", the urge to throw her hands above her head and shout her affliction for all to hear almost overwhelmed her. Twice she had visited a Pentecostal church in Agricola with Marion, and on both occasions the fervour of the congregation and the extraordinary effect produced on them by the hymn "The Lord's my shepherd, I'll not want" had frightened her. And the collapse of a young woman at the climax of the hymn,

> "For thine is the Kingdom
> And the power
> And the glory . . ."

brought home to her the gulf between her own world and that of Marion and Esther. Now, however, it was among that congregation that her spirit wandered, in search of that closer communion of which the first hymn had spoken.

An old woman next to her was singing lustily, as if her life depended on it. At the end of the service she asked Gladys if she was coming next Sunday.

"I think so."

"I come," declared the old woman, "when my feet can stand the walking."

The two walked for a while and then the old woman said, "I did know a woman who did look just like you, you know, years ago."

"Oh, yes?" asked Gladys.

"She din' last long though. Funny how people come and go, eh? She used to sit just where you is now. They bury her some time ago. I 'member the funeral good, you know. My memory in' gone yet. Not like some old people. It's the memory that give them trouble first. Eh, heh! Is the memory. But wha' fo' do? When is we time and the maker call us, that's it. Sometimes I wonder if we in' better off up there than down here, you know? Since my husband gone to his long home is only the church I got left. The children got they own troubles and you feel you in the way. Eh, heh! Is so. Eh, heh! You turning up this street? Me too. Is nice to meet people, you know, especially when they not stuck up. Like you, you not stuck up. I mean my husband was a fine, decent man and his grandfather was a teacher, you know. Mm hm! He come from a decent family, but they did come down in the world. But he was a

102

good man. Nowadays things different and people in' got so much time. Years ago people used to share whatever they had, but now everybody want to keep what they got for themselves. Is so, you know. But He don't change up there. He's the same now as he was a hundred years ago, and according to the Bible from the beginning of the world. You turning down here? All right. I goin' see you then. Walk good! Try and come next Sunday. Mm hm! All right. I walking down this road here."

That monologue did wonders for Gladys and when she got home she started to plan for the next day, the first when she would have to work as every range-yard woman was obliged to work. Only the washing would be given out, unless her husband objected, which was unthinkable.

After cutting up the wood into varying thicknesses and laying it beside the coalpot, Gladys swept the kitchen floor, filled the goblets with water, cleaned the children's shoes and washed the plates. She then put on the radio and sat down at the window. There she fell asleep and as her head nodded against her chest, woke up with a start.

The wind was rushing down the street, blowing bits of paper and shaking the trees violently. She looked up in anticipation of the storm, which broke a few minutes later, in a fury of rain and wind. Getting up she made certain that she had locked the back door; then she went back to bed, where she listened to the rain on the roof and the wind shaking the panes.

15

The Quarrel

When Armstrong discovered that Marion had left he abused his wife.

"I told you! I told you! You showed Esther the door and kept that whore. Now you know what retribution is. If you hadn't treated this girl like an equal, then she'd never have dared to give notice like that. Notice? She didn't even give notice, did she? My God! She even used to wear your clothes. Who ever heard of a servant wearing your clothes before you discarded them? In every house they eat in the kitchen after everybody else finished. But not your Marion! she owned the house and wanted wages and days off like these Georgetown fancy servants. She wanted to be treated like one of the family. If I'd have followed my mind you would've beaten her and sent her back to where she came from. What in God's name got into you? You didn't see your mother treating her servants like that, eh? And I bet they weren't bumptious with her!"

"No, they weren't," retorted Gladys.

"And you've become so damned submissive. As soon as I open my mouth you agree with me. You haven't got a mind of your own? I'll tell you this much, you're not having another servant. I can't afford to pay anybody. I don't know what's wrong with you. If you ask me you belong in an asylum."

"You're right, my friend," said Gladys wearily. "I belong there. You think I didn't know how you used to carry on with Marion at night? And in the same room as the children?"

"You're talking damn nonsense," replied Armstrong heatedly. "You see, you've even become suspicious. I told you you're going off. Go and ask your doctor. It's one of the signs of madness."

"It's your fault," she said quietly.

Armstrong lost his temper at the accusation and, with a swift movement of his arm, struck her a blow across the face.

104

"You can't hurt me any more," declared Gladys, "because I don't love you any more."

Armstrong, in order to hide his consternation and dismay at this unexpected disclosure, shouted at his wife:

"You're raving. You don't know even what you're saying any more."

Genetha had come upstairs for a saucer to put her mud cakes in. She went into the bedroom when she heard her parents quarrelling.

"If it wasn't for the children," said Armstrong, "I'd be out of here like a shot, you know," he said, doing his utmost to hurt her as much as he was able.

"I would stay with you always, my friend, because it's my duty."

Gladys's words, delivered with an apparent calm, cut deep into his vanity.

On hearing this exchange Genetha covered her head with the pillow and lay down on the bed.

"All right," said Armstrong vengefully, "I used to go with Marion. What did you expect? What sort of company're you? According to Marion you can't even stand your own children. Don't go pointing your finger at me, my girl! How can a man respect a wife who can't stand her own children, the children she brought into the world? I know your kind," he went on, in an attempt to cover up his shame at his own confession, "under your fine ways you're more brutal than the people who end up in prison. I mean, what sort of conversation I've had with you these last few years? If I shout at you you sulk for a week and when I try to be kind you reject me for it."

"God is my witness that I've been a good wife," she declared feelingly.

"God!" he shrieked. "God! Do you know about the minister and his wife? He's a man of God! He practically lives in God's house, as you call it. But it's common knowledge that he hasn't spoken to her for years."

"Who do you want me to call to witness, then?" asked Gladys. "I don't know anyone. If I haven't gone mad yet it's because I pray every day for your salvation and mine. Probably I could've been a better wife, but whenever I was ready to forgive you I couldn't bring myself to say what I wanted to say."

"Ready to forgive me for what?" enquired Armstrong. "There're men who drive their wives like slaves, that test the furniture with their finger to see if it's got dust on it; and ask them to account for the way they spend the money. Did I ever go poking into your purse or ask you how much a pair of shoes cost?"

Then, all of a sudden, his anger subsided and compassion for this woman, his wife for more than a dozen years, took its place. She was still attractive and gentle, the qualities that set her apart from her sisters. Why could they not start from the beginning, at least for the children's sake?

He looked at her from the corner of his eye and for the first time he thought he could detect a look of hatred in her eyes. And his resentment at this discovery was so strong that all the violence began to well up in his chest once more. He always complained that she was too submissive, but any display of independence or hostility put him into an indescribable fury.

Armstrong's denial that his wife was a desirable companion had injured her pride. Frightened at first by his angry outburst, Gladys was now prepared to face up to him. She looked him straight in the eye, while he made a heroic effort to restrain himself from saying all the things he knew would offend her.

"We've got two children and a home," she said, "and you've got a job when a lot of men haven't worked for months. Can't you try and make a go of things?"

He attempted to interrupt her, but she insisted.

"Let me talk, for God's sake! When you leave the house you don't tell me where you're going, and if anything happens to you I won't be able to say where you've been. And another thing: at least you could sit and talk to the children. The only thing you ever say to Boyie is to threaten him if he does badly at school and to flog him when he does something wrong."

Armstrong could contain himself no longer.

"Look who's talking about the children! At least I love my children."

"And do you think I don't!" she exclaimed.

Meanwhile Genetha had gone downstairs to tell Boyie that their parents were quarrelling. He was playing in the yard of

106

a friend who lived a few houses away. Disturbed at the news he came with her. When, on reaching the gate, he heard the shouting he turned to his sister and struck her on the back, angry that the news she had brought was correct.

Genetha seized the opportunity to intervene in the quarrel. Rushing up the stairs, she shouted, "Boyie cuffed me!"

Hearing this, Armstrong summoned Boyie from the yard, dragged him into the children's bedroom and thrashed him on his bare backside.

These events, which occurred in the space of a few minutes, filled Armstrong with great sadness. He brooded over his wife's words and wondered if it was in his power to put into practice her admonitions. How could he come close to his children when he did not know what to do? Could he stroke Genetha's head? When? On what pretext? The child would run away if he tried to be gentle with her. And Boyie? He was so proud and sensitive; could anyone imagine him responding to a stroking hand, except to bite it? If he were to take them out where would they go? Then he remembered a conversation between his wife's father and a friend.

"All fathers are repressors, like teachers," his father-in-law had said.

The recollection of this judgement comforted him somewhat. And, in fact, when he thought of his teachers and his own father, the objects he connected most readily with them were the cane and the belt.

Armstrong's wife had uncovered in her husband a host of guilty feelings whose existence he had never before suspected. The intemperate punishment of Boyie for a minor misdeed was evidence of a brutality that had nothing to do with his own nature. Yet, at the time, he felt he could not act otherwise. His friends and acquaintances knew him as a restrained person who never raised his voice, and the harlots he met in the Water Street brothel saw in him a considerate type, a gentleman. It was as if, at home, he was urged by some private devil to bare his teeth and snarl like a fierce dog.

16

Baby

Armstrong found it impossible to stay home for the remainder of the day. He took a shower and passed his cut-throat razor superficially over his face. When he was about to leave the house he went up to his wife in order to kiss her on the cheek by way of atonement, but at the last moment changed his mind, and simply bade her goodbye.

He set out on the long ride to Plaisance, where he knew that Doc spent his Sundays with his mother. Once in the village he had little difficulty in finding the house in which Doc's mother was supposed to live, behind the jamoon tree by the trench which rose above the vegetation like a sentinel.

Armstrong had to leave his bicycle leaning against the tree and cross the plank over the trench on foot.

After knocking on the door it occurred to him that it was foolish to ride all the way from Georgetown to Plaisance in the hot sun to see someone who might be somewhere else. Even if Doc were in Plaisance he was likely to be at a friend's house or to have gone visiting in the next village.

The door opened without the warning sound of footsteps and Armstrong found himself face to face with a wizened old lady. Without waiting to hear whom Armstrong had come to see she turned her head and shouted.

"Teacher! Is fo' you."

In saying this the old woman chuckled to herself, as if the visit were a joke.

A few moments later Doc appeared in pyjamas from the back of the two-roomed house, and when he saw Armstrong in the doorway he blinked in disbelief.

"Is you?"

Armstrong anwered with a gesture of embarrassment and stepped in from the sunlight.

"Man, you're the last person I expected to see down here," declared Doc. "I—I thought you were with your family, you

108

know. I thought at this time you'd all be dressed up and visiting with the family. . . ."

At this point the sound of female voices came from inside. Doc looked at Armstrong and smiled weakly and showed his friend the rocking-chair in the corner.

After Doc had disappeared inside, Armstrong sat alone in the drawing-room, surveying the walls, which were bare, except for photographs of married couples and little children. The two shutters were closed against the sun, streaming in through a chink between the window and the wall.

Armstrong felt as if he were sitting for ages, when out of the back came a striking looking woman in her twenties. She placed a bottle of rum and a glass in his hand and then drew up a straight-backed chair from the other side of the room on which to rest the rum bottle. She did not smile, but at the same time seemed quite friendly.

As the young woman disappeared into the back, Armstrong took the top off the bottle and poured himself a shot. He must have been alone for about half an hour by the time Doc reappeared. And despite the latter's neglect he was glad to be there. The strains of East Indian music came through the open door, the endless meanderings of a monotonous voice singing in Hindi. Occasionally people passed by on the village road, not caring to look through the open door. A dog was lying under a tree in the yard, sleeping with its legs in the air, stiff and twisted, as if it had died in that position. The vegetation growing beside the trench on the other side of the road was lush and deep green, dominated by a profusion of wild eddoe, and from time to time a light breeze sprang up and the leaves of the tree and the growth beside the trench would shudder and sway.

Doc returned clean-shaven and dressed in a sharkskin suit, and his hair was so liberally pomaded with Vaseline that he looked like a sweet man on a Saturday night.

If there had been a back door to the house Doc would have made the young woman leave when Armstrong arrived, for he could not entertain his friend out front while she stayed in the back all afternoon. However, now that the existence of his woman had been disclosed, Doc felt flattered that she was so attractive. The puritanical strain in his character had made him conceal the truth about his Sundays in Plaisance, but his man-of-the-world inclinations prevented him from going to any great lengths to keep his secret.

"To hell with it," he thought, "I'm not the only man in the country who's left his wife and is living with another woman."

In fact, Doc had been living a double life, teaching in Georgetown during the week, while spending his Sundays in Plaisance with a mistress he had known for three years. He was continually haunted by the thought of losing his livelihood if the Education Department or the manager of his school became aware of the facts of his private life. The manager of his school, a Methodist minister, considered him a fine man, whose only defect was the neglect of his soul. Furthermore, his wife in Berbice might get wind of his affair and she was not the sort to let sleeping dogs lie. It would be bad enough if she got hold of his address!

These thoughts only came to him when he was alone; but in the company of Baby and *mother*, far from the hurly-burly of Georgetown and the pressures of school life, he had learned to relax, walk around without a shirt and listen to conversations he would consider petty elsewhere. Often, in the late afternoon he, the old woman and Baby would sit on the steps without exchanging a word and the silence would be broken only by the greeting of a passer-by.

Baby was powerfully built. Her hips were round and her breasts full. She was barely literate and so ignorant that Doc's attempts at imparting to her an elementary knowledge of world affairs proved vain. In the presence of educated people Doc would rather she displayed her attractions with her mouth closed.

When Baby heard that someone had come to see Doc she felt a certain trepidation.

"Is what he want?" she had asked, as he came back into the bedroom.

"It's a friend of mine," he said, reassuring her.

He lifted up her dress and stroked her between the legs to show her that she was still his main preoccupation. And she watched him change, still harbouring the unease in her.

"Hey, take the big bottle and a cup for him. That's a good girl," he said, dispatching her with a slap on her buttocks.

Although she already disliked this man whom she had not yet seen properly she gave her hair a few strokes with a brush and smoothed her dress; and this concern for her appearance did not escape Doc, who, when she next addressed him, answered irritably. Their Sunday had already been spoiled by this man from town, she thought.

Doc went out to see Armstrong, clean-shaven and dressed in his usual immaculate way, and they got down to the business of consuming the obscure brand of rum.

On Saturday nights the friends drank only Russian Bear Black Label, smooth and rich. This cheap stuff had to be chased with soda water to put out the fires it kindled in a man's throat.

As they drank the two friends wondered what to say to each other.

"Rass!" thought Doc, "he didn't have to look for me down here."

Meanwhile, Armstrong was thinking that Doc was on to the sort of thing he had been after for years.

"He must be mad to ride all this way in the sun," thought Doc.

"My conscience would make me sick with worry, though," Armstrong reflected.

"Shit!" Doc said to himself, "we haven't even done it yet. If he doesn't go before seven o'clock that would be that, and I'd have to wait until next week again. A whole blasted week!"

"Doc, man, you're a first-class liar!" said Armstrong finally.

"I didn't lie, I just didn't mention her. I bet there's a lot you don't tell me. I bet you've got some little thing in Albouystown."

Armstrong was offended at the mention of Albouystown, the worst slum quarter in Georgetown. If he had a mistress she would certainly not be living in Albouystown.

"In fact," Doc continued, "you didn't tell B.A. and me anything, except that you're married and got two children. And your wife? What's she look like? I mean, you're damned secretive. You and B.A. know a lot about me. You know about my wife and my mother-in-law — may her soul rot in Hell.

You've been in my house, you know about my work and the people I work with. Now you know Baby, the ignorant bastard."

"Is that her name?" asked Armstrong.

Doc nodded. "When I'm sick it's Baby who's going to look after me, not the woman I went up to the altar with."

"If I was you I'd hurry up and get sick," quipped Armstrong.

The two friends laughed, Armstrong with his deep guffaw and Doc with his high-pitched, contagious laugh.

The women, encouraged by their laughter, came out and joined them, and as Armstrong and Doc occupied the only chairs they sat down on the top of the stairs. The sun was still hot, but the steps were in shadow and Baby and the old woman leaned on their elbows and looked across the trench, where a woman squatting by the water was beating her washing with regular strokes. Overhead, a carrion crow wheeled lazily under the steel-blue sky.

After the bottle had been drunk Doc pretended that there was no more left. He was at his most talkative and opened his heart to Armstrong.

"See that old hag on the steps. She's the one to watch. She's always egging Baby on to squeeze me. Thinks I've got a lot of money. The other day she was telling her that teachers get a lot of money, and now she's got Baby believing I'm rich. You've got to hand it to her, she can make money go far. But she's always complaining she's sick and she needs to go to the doctor. And if I open a bottle of rum I might as well finish it, 'cause she drinks it and on Sunday when I come she tells me some cock-and-bull story about leaving the bottle open and the rum evaporating. Would you believe it?"

Doc leaned forward and looked through the door.

"I'm telling my friend what you do with my rum," he called out.

Her only answer was to give him a suck-teeth, long and eloquent. And Armstrong listened, the smile on his face concealing his envy. He could tell from the way Doc was talking that he liked the old lady.

"He gat another battle in there," the old woman said, letting the cat out of the bag by way of revenge.

Doc, caught out, made the best of the situation.

"Why didn't you tell me?" he asked. "Well, go and get it, ne?"

Baby got up languidly and went inside to fetch the bottle of rum.

"You stingy bad, you know," the old woman said.

"You think I'm a money tree?" Doc defended himself.

Baby brought out the rum and broached it for the two men.

"I'm warning you," said Doc, "we'll have to drink the whole bottle now, 'cause she'll only finish it."

And in saying this he nodded in the old woman's direction.

"Don't bother with him, mister, I don' drink. I does drink, Baby?"

But Baby, as if struck dumb by the heat, did not answer, and the old woman delivered herself of another long suck-teeth.

"One Saturday," said Doc, "I came and found her sitting on the steps, smoking her clay pipe and drinking rum and ginger."

And then, addressing the old woman again, he said: "I thought you didn't drink!"

But she stood on her dignity and did not reply.

"She'd drink you and me under the table, I tell you," Doc pursued.

Doc had already forgotten that Armstrong had intruded in his Sunday nest and that he and Baby had not had time to make love. Indeed, what with the rum and the sun, he was glad that his friend had come to visit him, and hoped that he would stay till well into the night.

"A few months ago," he continued, "I bought Baby a second-hand machine, as an investment, mind you. She and the old hag fondled the thing and stroked it, but neither of the two knew how to use it. Baby promised to learn, but she still hasn't done anything about it. D'you know what the old lady wanted to do with the machine? Sell it! And she'd have sold it for more than I paid for it, I can tell you. She'd sell anything."

He laughed his uproarious laugh, then took out his handkerchief and wiped his eyes.

"And if you're not careful," he continued, "and you stand too long in one place, she'd sell you too, the old hag."

And at this observation he broke out into such a fit of laughter that he was obliged to hold his sides.

"Oh, God!" he exclaimed. "I laugh so much my sides hurting me."

He stopped talking in order to recover his breath and ease the pain in his sides. Armstrong refilled his glass and drank deeply from it.

In all his life he had never experienced such envy. He was jealous of Doc's association with Baby, of his relationship with the old woman, of his house in Plaisance. He felt that under the influence of the cane spirit he might commit an indiscretion. But he could not know that Doc's vanity had already interpreted his silence as envy, although he took care to pretend that he was not aware of it.

"Sometimes," said Doc, "I imagine myself with Baby in a boat on the river, with a bottle of rum in one hand and a book of poetry in the other. What does it matter if she understands what I'm reading or not, so long as she sits opposite me without talking, her legs slightly parted. Just slightly, so's not to spoil things. It's the suggestion, the promise. It's the difference between getting drunk on Russian Bear Black Label and on cheap rum like this. . . . I'm a *bad* man, I tell you, a *bad* man."

And he chuckled at his own words and the more refined implication of the word "bad".

"Beloved," he went on, "I shall love you like the wind and the sun and the driving rain. . . . Ah," he said, emptying his glass, "give me Baby any day for ten of your town women."

Armstrong felt a sudden urge to confess his unhappiness to his garrulous friend.

"You know," he said, "it was a mistake getting married. I'm not complaining, mind you, but it was a damned mistake."

He had blurted out the words, letting them go without really wanting to.

"You're not talking about yourself," said Doc, his display of merriment cut short by his friend's unexpected confession. "Look, you needn't. . . ."

114

And then, with a very serious air, he asked, "You're not in earnest?"

"I damn well am," replied Armstrong.

"What?"

"The thought of marrying into a Queenstown family, you know, when I was younger. What a mistake it is, marrying out of your class."

"She isn't unfaithful?" enquired Doc.

"No, nothing like that. Its just that I can't stand being home."

"Why?"

"The servant's gone," replied Armstrong, "and we can't afford anybody else. The boy's running wild and the wife's sick with worry. . . . The fact is, it's been always like that, since when we were living in Agricola."

Suddenly, he regretted having bared his soul to his friend, and Doc, sensing his embarrassment, started talking again, about something entirely different.

"It's a funny thing with some people, how they like talking about their small days. Old Schwarz at my school's a quiet sort of fellow. He'll sit with you all night drinking and hardly say a word. He'll listen and drink, listen and drink, as if it was a crime to mix in the conversation. But there's always one way to get Schwarz to talk. Let somebody mention small days and he'll smile and swallow the liquor as if it made out of water; and when he gets a chance he'll start off about his small days. And you'd think he was happy! Nothing of the sort. He used to live with his mother and father sometimes and at other times with his grandmother. When he was at his grandmother he used to pine away and think of home and when he was at home he used to threaten to run away to his grandmother. But you should hear this man talking about the jamoon trees by Clay and the bananas he and his brother used to steal from the farmer, and the days when the trench-water used to overflow into Capitol Cinema and they used to sit in the pit with their feet in water. And when he was done he would take a long drink and fall silent for the rest of the night."

Doc emptied his glass and called out to Baby.

"Girl, get us another bottle. There's two more under the

bed, unless the old woman did drink them already, the sly, old hag."

"I thought you din' had any more," grunted the old woman. "You tell the man you din' got any more and now you talking 'bout the two under the bed. You see how he is, mister? He so stingy he would make monkey look like a wastrel. What about a new dress, ne?"

She got up and lifted up her dress to the knees.

"Look at this thing! Call this a dress? You in' shame to bring a stranger here when I look like this?"

"We see it, we see them," Doc said, with a look of disgust.

Her shrivelled legs were so skinny Doc was moved to remark, "That's the two wonders of the world. How those legs manage to hold up that body no man'll ever know."

Baby came back out with the rum and placed the bottle on the table. She then went inside once more for a kerosene lamp, which she hung on a nail, by the door.

"That's all right?" she asked.

"That's all right, girl," Doc answered.

Armstrong noticed the glint in her eye and felt the jealousy welling up in him once more.

"She's nice, eh?" Doc remarked. "You want a go?" he then asked mischievously.

Armstrong lowered his eyes and did not reply, although the suggestion made the blood rush to his face. If Doc had not really meant it he would look like a fool if he took him seriously. It was best to say nothing, he thought. And Doc did not fail to notice that his friend was following the girl with his eyes whenever she came in and left the room; he was such a fool, he thought.

"Nobody understands himself or his own troubles," Doc continued. "Everybody's making frantic efforts to get out of some deep pit. If it's not a husband or a wife or a mother-in-law behind them it's a boss or a neighbour or a father or son. There's always a tormentor kicking you back into the pit. From Monday to Friday I'm alone. I haven't got anyone in this bastard world but Baby. Well, it's the kiss-me-ass truth. If my radio breaks down I feel as if I'm going mad. I've got to get it repaired right away so's not to have to spend the nights

116

alone. There's nothing worse than having to drink in a rum shop. It's not that I don't understand you, but I'll tell you, it's better to be unhappily married than to be single."

Doc felt that he had spoken the truth, but at the same time he was convinced that his weekends with Baby and his outings with Armstrong were ample compensation for his bachelor existence. He was the sort of man who could strike up an acquaintanceship in a cake shop or find someone to replace Baby if the need arose. He was in love with her and believed her indispensable to his way of life; but, in truth, he was persuaded that she would suffer more in the event of an estrangement than he.

"Light the lamp, ne?" Doc called out to Baby, who had joined the old woman on the step.

"Leave the child!" exclaimed the old woman. "You only showing off in front of you friend."

But Baby got up from the step and lit the lamp, which she replaced on the nail.

It had become dark and the lamp did little except cast shadows round it. The frogs had meanwhile started up a chorus of incessant croaking from the trench, choked with algae and wild hyacinth; and the evening was as warm as the day had been so that the women, sitting on the stairs, did not think it necessary to come inside. All the hens and the solitary cock which had been pecking about the yard all afternoon had disappeared into the back yard, where they had no doubt found some place to roost for the night. The East Indian music which came from deeper in the village took on a more ample sound in the waxing night, and, with the frogs, accompanied the conversation of the two men. Both had no more thought for time, and even Doc, annoyed at first that his love-making might have been spoiled by Armstrong's visit, was only concerned at keeping his friend with him as long as possible. In any case he was in no condition to do justice to his manhood in bed.

"He goin' be so drunk you goin' to put he in bed. I telling you!" said the old woman, addressing no one in particular.

"He might as well stay the night," Baby said.

"You can talk!" exclaimed the old woman, sucking her teeth so loudly that the men heard her.

"What's eating you now?" asked Doc. "If you're hungry why don't you go down and buy something from Fung-kee-Fung, ne?"

And saying this Doc took out a dollar note from his pocket and tended it to her.

"You know he shut now," she said.

"Knock on his back door, then," Doc suggested pretending to be exasperated with her.

The old woman got up slowly, trying to hide her pleasure at the windfall. She might as well spend the whole dollar note while he was drunk, she thought. And she left immediately for the shop, barefooted.

Armstrong heaved a deep sigh.

"You want some liqour, girl?" he asked Baby.

"No, I in' eat yet. After I eat."

"Come here let Armstrong feel your batty," Doc told her, stretching out his hand.

Pouting with displeasure she came over to Doc, who stroked her backside theatrically.

"Feel it, man. Come on!" he urged Armstrong.

Doc's guest allowed his hand to be guided by his host and to explore the contours of Baby's backside.

"That's a batty and a half and a piece 'pon top, eh?" Doc asked.

"You friend shy," Baby ventured.

"You see that?" Doc said, laughing heartily.

But despite his laughter Doc was not pleased at Baby's compliance.

"It's time you think about going home, man," he told Armstrong. "What's your wife going to say?"

Then to Baby he said, "You know these married men. After a bit on the side they rush home to their wives with black pudding and nut cake."

Baby smiled as if she understood and Armstrong got up, wavered on his feet and fell back into the chair.

"Come on, come on, you got to get going," Doc encouraged him.

He and Baby helped him down the stairs. Then Doc took his bicycle to the public road, while Baby held his arm. And

Armstrong, despite his condition, was aware of her body rubbing against his arm and wanted to go back to the house.

"We can't go back?" he asked her.

"Is what your wife goin' say?" she asked in return.

They skirted the trench, crossed the railway line and at last reached the Public Road, where Armstrong and Doc went behind some trees to relieve themselves.

"That was good," Doc said, as he shook his penis behind his tree.

Baby heard them laughing and wondered what they were laughing about. When they emerged from the darkness they were both buttoning their trousers, oblivious of their lack of propriety in the young woman's presence.

Doc and Baby waved to Armstrong as he mounted his bicycle and rode off in the direction of town.

"Once he mounts that bicycle he's all right. He can even sleep on it," Doc told her.

"You going have to stay the night," Baby told him, with obvious satisfaction.

"I know, girl. I'm going to drink a cup of cocoa and go to bed."

And the two walked back to the house, hand in hand, like young lovers.

Doc lay on the bed, listening to the women talk about goings on in the village. Bagwadeen's baby was sick with thrush and the nurse had promised to come, but had not turned up. Ramoo's wife had run away. Her father pleaded with her husband to go and look for her, but he refused and swore that if she did not return the following day he would have back the cow he gave him before the wedding. Doc soon fell asleep, bemused by the rum and indistinct memories of the session he had just shared with his friend.

17

A Malignant Growth

Armstrong heard from an acquaintance that B.A. had been taken to hospital with a malignant growth. He rode off to see Doc in Kitty that very afternoon to tell him what he had learnt and they went to the hospital at once.

B.A. was in the paupers' ward on the first floor of the immense complex of wooden buildings. Dressed like the other pauper ward inmates in a white garment that came down to his ankles, he was standing next to his narrow bed, as if awaiting some kind of inspection.

"Somebody tell me someone been enquiring for me," B.A. said cordially, but without smiling.

He got back into bed once the formalities were over.

"Now you know why I was always so irritable," he said apologetically.

"What is it exactly?" Doc asked, putting his arm round his sick drinking companion.

"Cancer. You didn't hear? They call it a malignant growth. Same thing. . . ."

"I don't know what to say, old war horse," Armstrong remarked, trying to hide his emotion.

"Don't say anything," B.A. ordered.

And then, to break the silence, he recalled how he was attacked by the masked masqueraders on Christmas Eve night some years before.

"They attacked the right one," he said jokingly. "I didn't have a cent on me."

Visitors were sitting on chairs and on the beds or were standing at the patient's bedsides, while the nurses — even without their uniforms — would have been conspicuous by their purposeful walk. There was the scent of sweet oranges in the air, and on looking round him Armstrong saw the fruit laid in twos and three on the beds of a number of patients. Some of the visitors were poised for flight — or so it seemed to Armstrong. Perhaps it was his own sense of discomfort he could read on their faces; but the fact was that a number of them were standing beside empty chairs.

Armstrong considered his neglect of B.A. in the past and his unconcealed preference for Doc. If he saw his own son behaving in a similar way he would speak to him of the need to consider the feelings of others. But he had behaved like that, without thinking.

The sight of B.A., dressed in a neutral garment of white, surrounded by innumerable beds in a vast ward like rafts on a windless sea, distressed him even more than his fatal illness.

"There's a man in here," said B.A., "who hops around. I mean it. He doesn't walk, he hops!"

"Hops?" asked Doc eagerly, anxious to make up for his part in the quarrel at the cake shop in Kitty.

"He puts his legs together," explained B.A. "and hops about. Somebody says that's how he used to get about even before he came into hospital; and the traffic had to stop to wait for him to cross the road. One of the doctors says he's got a castration fear. Hm! Or, he said, it could be he want to draw people's attention to his troubles. But you know what I think? I think he does hop about because he likes hopping about."

Both Doc and Armstrong smiled.

"If you wait," said B.A. "you'll see him come into the ward and cause confusion. But the nurses let him have his way."

Doc and Armstrong exchanged glances.

"I don't like this promiscuity," remarked B.A. emphatically. "Just 'cause I don't have a family they don't have to put me—"

"What about your son?" asked Doc, deliberately interrupting him.

B.A. did not answer at once.

"I hear his woman's already moved in," he said after a while, "in the three days I've been in here. . . . Sensible when you come to think of it, with the housing shortage being what it is. But they could've waited a li'l space of time, a decent space of time. After all, my smell must still be clinging to the walls and the bedclothes. . . . There's an Amerindian in here, from the bush, with a broken back. He comes from Paramakatoi. Every morning before anybody's up he plays his flute, three notes, just three notes haunting the place . . . bringing all that bush sadness into the hospital as if we don't got enough of it in town. And you know the nurses don't stop him either. They allow the patients to do as they like. It won't surprise me to wake up one morning and find them running the hospital."

Armstrong and Doc could not know that B.A. was acutely put out by their visit. He detested their show of sympathy and would have preferred them to stay away. Besides, contrary to the impression he gave, he had already made friends with one of the patients and was not certain that he did not prefer it to his freedom. He talked to hide his embarrassment and his resentment at the way Doc had treated him the last time they met. He resented their good health and the fact that when visiting time came to an end they would be able to get up and leave with the army of visitors.

"We came empty-handed," observed Armstrong. "You see? Everybody brought something, but we came empty-handed. Next time we'll bring a whole basket of oranges."

"I can't stand them," declared B.A. gruffly.

And wounded by the unexpected rebuff Armstrong did not pursue the matter.

The hum of voices emphasised the silence between the friends, and Doc, affecting an interest in the activity around him, glanced at the clock on the wall.

Finally, it was time to go when, amid the goodbyes and the voices of nurses calling out the time, there was a loud "Ha, ha!" from the other side of the hall. In the doorway stood a man, stock-still, his hands raised high above his head and his gaze directed at his feet. Then, when all eyes were on him, he started off across the hall in little, careful hops, his legs together. He made his way between the beds and among the visitors, who stood watching him as if he were on a stage.

"All right, all right!" a young nurse called out. "Time to go. It's time."

And the visitors only went reluctantly, most of them turning at the doorway to look back at the progress of the man across the room, who stopped occasionally so as to recover his balance.

"And when you think," said B.A. bitterly, "that he's going nowhere!"

"We'll come and see you tomorrow," promised Doc. "And we'll bring the oranges all the same, because we know you like them."

"See you then," said B.A., who stood up and shook their hands in turn, just as if Doc and Armstrong were strangers to him.

"Hey," B.A. shouted after them when they were already at the top of the staircase, "those men in the masks who attacked me — the masqueraders — they had your build . . . and the one who shouted at me sounded just like you, Doc."

But they both pretended not to hear the insult hurled after them.

"I think we should go round to his house and talk to his son," suggested Armstrong. "All he needs is a visit from him."

"Have you ever spoken to him?" Doc asked.

"No."

"If you had you wouldn't have made the suggestion. He's the nastiest young person you'll probably ever meet, you've got my word for it."

That settled the matter.

Walking slowly the two men set off for their cake shop in Kitty, as if by a prearranged agreement. Ahead of them the electric lamp posts stretched, with their outgrowth of metal lamps connected by black wires that dipped at mid-point and rose again towards the lamp-post further on.

It was an evening like so many others, darkness falling rapidly and the houses by the roadside competing with the street lamps to lighten the gloom. Passing cars blew their horns indiscriminately and the occasional bus trundled by, brilliantly lit up, like a ponderous intruder of the night, giving an un-impeded view of its passengers.

Armstrong reflected that his friendship with Doc and B.A., imperfect as it was and marred by frequent quarrels, was the constant source of pleasure in his life. It was precisely the element that was lacking in his wife's, however; and if, while they were living in Agricola, he could pretend that the lack was the fault of their isolation, that excuse was no longer tenable, for he actively discouraged the association with his sister, who, living just under them, might have turned out to be her constant and good companion.

They were walking past a photographer's parlour and the pictures displayed in the window recalled the afternoon of their marriage, when he managed to get hold of one of the new motor cars to take them to the street photographer. She and he stood side by side as a knot of passers-by looked on. How proud he had been to be seen in her company! She was his possession and would spend a lifetime serving him, attending to his needs, anticipating his wishes. Everyone looking on must know that. He could not complain that she had let him down in any way. Indeed it was her mute resignation that took the taste out of their marriage.

"Did you hear what he said?" asked Doc, interrupting Armstrong's reflections.

"B.A.?"

"Yes."

"When?" asked Armstrong.

"As we were going down the stairs," Doc replied.

"I heard him shout," said Armstrong, not wishing to admit that he had heard B.A.'s insult.

"He said something like, 'he sounded just like you, Doc!'"

"You think we should have gone back?" Armstrong asked.

"He sounded vexed to me. Not to you?"

"You're sure he said 'Doc'?" enquired Armstrong. "He might've been shouting at somebody else."

"I heard the word 'Doc' distinctly," said Doc. "And you saw how he reacted when you offered to bring him oranges."

"For God's sake, don't let him drag you down with him," said Armstrong impatiently.

They walked on until they reached the street in which Doc lived.

"I think I'll have an early night," Doc said.

"You're going to see him tomorrow?"

"Why not?" Doc said. "Words never killed anybody."

The two friends separated; and Armstrong, finding himself

alone in the street, so many streets from home, was taken with a sudden desire to go and see Lesney.

He set off quickly, walking faster and faster, then breaking into a trot a hundred yards on. In the end he was running as fast as he could along the pavement, his loose jacket flapping at the sides. From time to time he came onto the road to avoid colliding with someone, but quickly regained the safety of the pavement, so as to get out of the way of a carriage or of the odd bus. Then, seized with a sudden shame, he slowed down to a walk.

"What in the name of God is wrong with me?" he thought. "If *she* knew! A father and husband!"

And his conduct seemed so absurd he turned up a side street to hide from anyone who might read his thoughts.

Wasn't everything absurd? he reflected. The work others did he was incapable of doing, just as his occupation was a mystery to others. He did not choose to be born, just as he was unable to choose the moment he was going to die. The things he wanted most were beyond his grasp and whatever was within his reach appeared pale and insignificant. He was despised by his son and had just been cursed by his sick friend. Tomorrow would be a day of gestures like the days before, and some night he would weaken and sink back into the earth without the consolation of gratitude from his children, whose affection suddenly appeared infinitely desirable.

And there appeared to Armstrong a vision of himself lying on a bed, arms crossed on his chest, being stared at by his wife's relations, his father-in-law and mother-in-law, and his two sisters-in-law who were grinning down at him. Without warning they both bent over and placed flowers on his eyes, on his cheeks and on his mouth, yellow daisies that grew in profusion by the roadside. And the elder of the two opened the buttons of his trousers and started to fondle him, smiling all the while and reassuring him. She kept whispering words to him, unintelligible at first, but becoming more and more distinct.

"It was the same in Agricola, when you brought me the pears," she kept repeating to him. "Try and remember. It'll be so beautiful, just as it was then."

And he closed his eyes and felt her warm hand round his ungodly erection.

"So you cared in Agricola?" he asked her, rising from his bed.

"Just sleep," she answered softly.

And in an explosion of stars he fell back and found himself alone in the dark room.

Armstrong was roused by the sound of an approaching carriage, but the unwonted weakness in his knees caused him to lean against the balustrade of the stone culvert.

Hoping that no one would pass he tried to pull himself together. It would not do to be taken home by strangers, as if he were drunk and helpless: that sort of thing never failed to reach the ears of one's superiors.

He was not sure what had happened to him, but he had had a similar *experience* when he was a youth and, fatigued and hungry, he arrived home to find that all the family were out.

And he remembered a curious conversation between his father and a fisherman friend, who took his boat out every night in search of queriman and snapper, and whose eternal complaint was that the fishermen had to go out further and further to obtain a worthwhile haul. One afternoon he overheard him telling his father that people who went out on the sea were not as certain of things as others were.

"Nothing's certain out there," the man had said. "Sometimes the trade winds that supposed to blow in one direction all the time does swing round, without no storm, nothing. And one night we haul up the net and what you think we find inside? Something looking just like a man, but with webbed feet."

Those words had aroused something slumbering deep within Armstrong, which he could share with no one else. It was as if someone inside him had spoken, uttering hidden feelings. And this second experience, the one he had just had, far from frightening him, had comforted him, reassuring him, as it were, of the continued existence of an inward companion, who was still capable of asserting his presence.

At last he was on his way home, certain that no one had been watching him. The streets appeared new and clothed in a wondrous, diaphanous material; and if the familiar houses had suddenly burst into fruit he would not have been astonished. And if the young woman coming towards him had stopped and spoken to him familiarly or embraced him he would not have thought that out of the way either.

Armstrong was convinced that the experience by the culvert had dissipated the uncertainties about relations with his family. From now on he would march through life with firm steps, confident of his strength and of his companion's within him.

18

Retrenchment

The wind of fear was blowing through the post office and government departments. One morning Armstrong received a letter informing him that one of the employees was to be pensioned off. The man, Armstrong's closest associate, was usually left in charge of the post office whenever Armstrong was away.

He thrust the letter in his pocket and that night lay awake thinking how he could help his deputy. And the next day the deputy, who had that morning received his letter confirming the information already communicated to Armstrong, came to him, dumbfounded by the news. He promised to get in touch with the Postmaster General, knowing full well that the decision would not be reversed.

Armstrong did as he had promised. He telephoned the Postmaster General's office and had to endure a rebuff. His deputy's dismissal was none of his business.

Armtrong's own dismissal occurred three months later, being communicated to him by a similar letter to the one his deputy had received. Retrenchment was in full swing.

That night he told Gladys and they sat in the gallery, reflecting on the news.

"Where're you going?" he asked wearily, as Gladys got up.

"To warm up your dinner," she replied.

"I wonder if you know what's going to happen?" he asked.

"We'll manage somehow. There's some good news. I was keeping it as a surprise."

"What?"

"Boyie's won a scholarship," she said.

"To where?"

"Progressive High School."

"They must be crazy," declared Armstrong. "He's never had a good report in his life, except the last one, and that wasn't particularly good."

"Look. If things get too bad we can always send Genetha to learn to sew and buy a sewing-machine out of your savings."

"A sewing-machine?" he repeated, chuckling to himself, recalling Doc's remarks about the machine he had bought for Baby.

"What's funny about that?" Gladys asked him.

"Nothing," Armstrong said, "it's just that we sold the one we had in Agricola," and his face fell. Then, bitterly, he exclaimed, "A sewing-machine!"

"Anyway," said Gladys, "the scholarship's a big problem out of the way."

And, for the first time in months Armstrong lost his temper.

"What's the point of getting a scholarship if you're starving?" he asked.

Gladys felt for him in a way she no longer thought possible. He seemed much older and more vulnerable.

"It's not the end of the world, you know," she said, trying to comfort him.

He would have to sell the two houses, he thought. Now he was in the position his sister found herself some time back, without an adequate income and only a little capital with which to eke out a meagre existence.

Armstrong, like most men, had no idea to what extent he was dependent on his work. His colleagues, the routine, even the scent of ink were as indispensable to him as the oxygen he breathed. He had often cursed the regular hours he was obliged to keep and persuaded himself that this, together with the routine, had thwarted his initiative and robbed him of his imagination. Yet, at the moment, he was as frightened of being cut off from his post office as he was of losing his salary. To get up early in the morning when the rain was pelting down and to don raincoat and galoshes, muttering all the while under his breath, was, after all, a sweet experience. Discrepancies in accounts, lost telegrams, letters of reproof from above, all these were the pinpricks that rendered life all the more attractive.

Furthermore, he believed he was indispensable to the proper functioning of his post office. There were things a new man could never understand. Nothing was more complex, nothing demanded a cooler head than the successful running of a post office, especially with the calibre of youngsters being recruited these days. And even if a man were educated, he might be dishonest. The country must be going to the dogs if people like himself were not to be allowed to continue in their jobs. The trouble with those in authority was that they never knew what was happening anywhere else except at the top. They sat on their fat tails and gave orders without any idea of the consequences that might follow.

Suddenly he was stricken with a fierce jealousy of his friend Doc. The worst that could happen to teachers was a cut in salary. Living alone, with few responsibilities, he could indulge his lecherousness as long as his body permitted. He, Armstrong, could not even afford to spend an hour with Lesney now.

Armstrong and his wife ate late that night. She watched him holding his head in his hands, bent over the steaming plate of pepperpot which, in Doc's words, was the queen of dishes, the one justification for imprisoning women in the home.

"Damn him! Damn him!" he exclaimed in an outburst incomprehensible to his wife.

They sat for hours in silence, until Boyie shouted out in his sleep, when his mother remarked with a touch of pride in her voice, "That boy!"

In the end Armstrong got up and went inside, leaving his wife to ponder over their future.

Everybody was surprised that Boyie had won a scholarship. Boyie, however, knew exactly why he had won it, and the moment that, a year ago, he had set out to be first in his class. It was the occasion of somebody's jubilee, when pencils were being shared out to the top half of the class; and when he received a pencil there was an outcry from the other children.

"Boyie work not good, miss," one child remarked.

Miss Caleb looked over to the seat where he was sitting and declared amidst silence, "Boyie got a pencil because I like him."

It was as if a thunderbolt had struck Boyie. This, for him, was a declaration of love from his teacher, an open announcement of favouritism. He therefore returned this passion with commendable swiftness. From that day onwards school was a beautiful place, and Arithmetic, the mysteries of long division and area, furnished the excuse to take his work to be marked. He asked his mother to test him on his tables, to give him subjects for composition which he might write out with a pencil on Saturday nights. And his progress was so striking that Miss Caleb took his work to the headmaster as proof of her teaching ability; for poor, pock-marked Miss Caleb did not realise that she haunted Boyie's dreams and fired his enthusiasm during his waking hours.

One afternoon, on the way home from school he told his best friend, Ashmore, of his love for Miss Caleb.

"But she ugly!" he remarked.

Boyie stopped, a pained expression on his face. He looked at Ashmore as if he had said something disparaging about his, Boyie's mother.

"What wrong with you?" Ashmore asked, puzzled.

And in answer Boyie gave him a blow on the chin with a violent swing of his right fist. Ashmore lost his balance and fell on the wet pavement, astonished at his friend's behaviour. Boyie was aggressive, but until then, he and Ashmore had always fought on the same side; attacking each other was unthinkable. Ashmore grabbed Boyie's legs and pulled him to the ground and the two friends rolled into the gutter, belabouring each other.

A crowd of school children and a few adults gathered round them, the children shouting encouragement to both boys.

"Get he, boy; get he!"

"Tek he by he foot!"

"Put you foot round he neck an' bruck he neck!"

"Cuff he in he belly!"

"That's right, Ashmore, squeeze he eye out!"

"Stan' up and fight, man, like Tom Keene!" said a grown man, an admirer of the film star.

"Grab he by he balls!" one big boy shouted ecstatically.

Ashmore must have followed this last bit of advice, for at that moment Boyie let out a shriek which attracted even more passers-by. One burly man took the two boys by the scruff of their necks and lifted them up bodily. He then let go and shouted, "Police!" and the crowd vanished like water down a sink, with Boyie and Ashmore hard behind those fleeing down Regent Street. The burly man grinned broadly and went on his way.

Boyie had fought for Miss Caleb and had had his balls squeezed for Miss Caleb. He was now ready to lay down his life for her and, while waiting for the call, he slaved away for her.

If Boyie had worked with such application from his Infant School days onwards he would have run away with the Primary School scholarship. Instead, his energies and anxieties had been channelled into mischief, into making life unpleasant for his mother at weekends.

He often wished his father would take him out kite-flying or to cock fights, as his friends' fathers did. He was hardly at home to witness the trouble Boyie caused his mother. A word from his father and he would have shown all those clowns in his class what it meant to be bright. None of them could beat him at marbles and most of them could not even hold a cricket bat properly, while he played in the fields with boys from secondary schools and could late cut a good length ball. None of them even knew what a good length ball was. Did they really think there was much difference between school work and cricket? Only teachers did, and they had as much sense as a stinking toe. Except Miss Caleb, of course. He decided to get to the top of his class and win the Primary scholarship for her.

The last day of term Boyie met Miss Caleb in front of the school and put her hand on his head.

"I'll miss you," she said, then turned away and left him standing alone by the wall.

And standing there he burst into tears, all of a sudden, without knowing why.

That night while he lay in bed he experienced the most shameful fantasies about Miss Caleb. As he ran his hand through her hair she covered his face with kisses, gathered him up in her arms and pressed him to her.

Boyie woke up and found his mother bending over him.

132

"Son, you're all right?"

"Yes, Mother," he answered.

"You've been muttering to yourself."

"It's nothing."

"You were dreaming?"

"I suppose so."

"You want me to stay with you?" his mother asked.

"No," he answered hurriedly.

She bent down to kiss him good night, but he quickly turned his head away.

His mother left the room and Boyie recalled the night when he saw his father and Marion embracing in the dark. He had never told anyone; he had never felt like telling anyone. But the secret was painful, and early the next morning, when everyone was asleep, he got up and searched for Marion's dress in the dark. He tried to rip a hole in it, but could not manage to undo the seam. And while he was looking round for something else of hers to destroy she woke up and asked him what he was doing.

"Is none of your business," he answered.

From then on he went to any lengths to inconvenience and annoy her, and he once told a boy at school that he wanted to die because he did not like their servant.

St Barnabas school, with its dingy walls and anxious teachers, had no idea what an impression it had made on young Armstrong who often had been condemned as a delinquent and caned as a rebellious spirit; who, except in his last year, possessed not even the saving grace of an agile mind; St Barnabas, where the powerful symbols of the cross and the cane nudged each other intimately. Yet Boyie, whenever he recalled St Barnabas, saw neither the cross nor the cane, but a dark hand on his forehead.

19

A Visit

If Gladys Armstrong had pretended not to be unduly worried about the future, in order to assuage her husband's fears, she was none the less as frightened as he was. What sort of pension would he receive? The proceeds of the sale of the houses would not last long and Armstrong would be too proud to take a menial job. As things were they were finding it difficult to make ends meet and she dreaded the thought that one of them might fall ill and end up in the paupers' ward of the Public Hospital. Perhaps one of the children could go and live with her parents; but she knew that her husband would never allow it. She herself could turn her hand to nothing, since her only talent was doing intricate embroidery, and playing the piano; and Armstrong had never thought it necessary to buy a piano. With the money from the houses they could well open a shop of some description; but she shuddered at the idea of standing behind a counter, dispensing wares to customers.

Armstrong would suffer most of all. He would have to forego the new clothes he liked so much and, at table, he would have to be content with what everyone else was eating. If Esther were still with them she would find some way of bringing money into the home. A business would flourish under her skilled guidance and the problem of who would sell behind the counter would be solved as well. But how was Esther to be found in a big town like Georgetown?

When Armstrong came home that afternoon she told him what she had in mind, but to her surprise he threw cold water on the plan at once.

"What you know about business?" he asked. "You know as much as me."

"Why not give it a chance, Sonny? Do you know of anyone who started a business and ended up poor?"

"Who you mean? Most of them are poor, these shop-keepers," Armstrong replied, but was interrupted by his wife.

"It doesn't have to be a cake shop," countered Gladys.

"Tcha! You don't even know what you're talking about."

Gladys gave up, bewildered by his lack of enterprise. Above all she was thinking of Boyie and the possibility of his education being cut short because they could not afford to keep him in shoes and shirts.

"I know it's Boyie you're worried about," Armstrong told her. "But the scholarship will pay for his school fees and if we can't buy books he can always sponge on his friends. I can tell you, that's the least of my worries."

"And what about Genetha?" Gladys asked.

"She's a girl," he said with a deprecating gesture, "and besides, you yourself said we can buy a machine for her and let her do sewing."

"And you'll buy the machine?"

Armstrong hesitated. "I'll have to wait and see. When you come to think of it a machine is expensive. I mean it's no use buying her one of these cheap second-hand things."

"Why not?" Gladys asked.

"For a start it won't last."

And in a desperate attempt to make her husband see reason Gladys went to look up her father and ask him to speak with Armstrong.

The old man pretended to drop in one night to find out how the family were getting on, and feigned surprise when he was told by Armstrong that he would be soon on pension. These were hard days and only a lucky few were in jobs that paid them a full salary. What would Armstrong do?

Flattered by his father-in-law's concern he disclosed that he would be selling his houses to tide them over the next two years until something turned up.

That was risky, thought Gladys's father, since all the experts thought that the recession would be a long one. Could he not buy a business?

Armstrong at once understood what had happened. He looked at his wife, who pretended to be absorbed in her darning.

"Business isn't for me," he told his father-in-law. "I'd only make a mess of it."

The older man realised that he could not mention Esther

without letting the cat out of the bag, so used other arguments to persuade Armstrong that business was the only way to beat the depression.

"You could even end up a rich," the older man remarked half jokingly.

When Gladys's father was ready to go, Armstrong said that he would accompany him home. But he declined his invitation to go into his house which looked no different from the way it did nearly fifteen years ago, except that it needed painting.

Slowly he made his way back down New Garden Street, looking up at the fine houses and admiring the large gardens in front of them, in which flourished roses and dahlias, their stalks maintained by a staff to which they were tied. In the midst of misery this was how some people lived, he thought. It could not be right. In front of one house several cars were parked and he could hear the hum of conversation coming from the well-lit gallery, where people were standing with glasses in their hands. He stood in front of this house, which was decorated with fixed jalousies and a wrought-iron grill below a line of windows. If he invested in a business would all this be within his grasp? Many businesses had had small beginnings. Suppose he were to lose everything? The thought kept recurring to dampen his aspirations and he could only see the obstacles, the hard work and the pains he would have to take to make the venture a success.

And Armstrong decided once and for all that business was not for him.

20

Age and Remorse

One evening Doc and Armstrong decided, after another visit to the paupers' ward, to leave their houses early the next morning and go to the groin for an early morning swim. Doc was agreeably surprised when Armstrong suggested he should pick him up at the house.

It was the start of the Christmas school holidays, a lonely season for him, and the invitation was like an unexpected gift. Armstrong had never before invited him in and had only once spoken about his family, on that afternoon in Plaisance when he was not entirely responsible for what he said.

As Doc knocked on Armstrong's door he tried to visualise the features and build of his wife, for he assumed that it was she who would open for him. But when the door opened it was Armstrong who stood in the doorway.

"Come in and meet my wife," he suggested.

Doc took a seat and waited for his friend to come back, marvelling all the while at the silence in the house, for he himself would have called out for his wife if it had been his home.

The drawing-room had a faded elegance and its wicker chairs and easy chairs were decorated with coloured cushions. Its walls were almost bare, except for a large sepia photograph of Armstrong that dominated the partition dividing it from a bedroom. A handsome oil-lamp capped by a decorated, opaque globe recalled the twenties, a decade ago, when many of the houses had yet to be provided with electricity.

The thought occurred to Doc that in that kind of house and with that sort of woman, who was capable of maintaining such a home, his ambitions in the teaching profession would surely have been realised.

Accompanied by an almost inaudible rustling of cloth Gladys Armstrong was suddenly upon him, smiling and hand outstretched.

"I've heard so much about you," she said. "Why didn't you come before?"

And Doc jumped up to take her hand.

"Oh," he stuttered, not knowing what to say.

She sat down opposite him.

"Sonny said you're swimming this morning. Perhaps you'd like to have breakfast with us afterwards."

"I'd very much like to," Doc said, "but it'll have to be another time. I'm going to Plaisance after the swim . . . to look up some people."

"What a pity," she said, with such sincerity that Doc was touched.

Armstrong came out once more, carrying a bag with his swim suit and a towel.

Gladys got up and followed them on to the porch, where she stayed to wave after them. And Doc, as he turned away from the house, would have liked to go back and tell her how he appreciated the way he was received.

"Well, I never!" was all he could manage to say as he walked by Armstrong's side along the road.

"How d'you mean?" asked Armstrong.

"You don't deserve a woman like that, that's all."

Armstrong made no reply but was none the less flattered, for his vanity prevented him from grasping the full import of Doc's remark.

Doc reflected that there was more that Armstrong could have told him about his wife. She seemed ill to him. But maybe she was the type, fleshless, but full of vitality.

And Armstrong's friend's observation about Gladys's appearance had not missed the mark. For several days she had been suffering from dizzy spells, but had said nothing, for fear of alarming her husband.

It was December. The rains had come soon and fell so vehemently Gladys had the feeling that she was living in a drum. To her dismay a leak appeared in the bedroom, over the bed in which she and Armstrong slept, so she moved it and put down a bucket to catch the water.

She had just finished the sweeping and had not yet begun

138

to cook the midday meal. The woman who did the washing had been up to ask if she could hang the clothes to dry under the house, for the rain prevented her from hanging them out in the range-yard where she lived. Gladys agreed, though she suspected that not only her clothes would be hung up, but the clothes of other families for whom the woman washed. Armstrong would almost certainly be angry when he found out; but the washerwoman was one of the most capable in the area and the clothes were always delivered on time, clean and bug-free. They were neither over-starched nor under-starched, and one had the impression that the Chinese laundry could not provide a better service.

What with such problems and the endless housework Gladys began to long for a protracted sleep, free of worry. Where could her husband find a man to repair the roof at little cost? This was the first month of his retirement and the washerwoman would have to be paid out of their savings. There was no doubt now but Genetha would have to leave school and relieve her mother of some of the housework. These thoughts scurried through her mind as she washed and picked the rice. Neither she nor Genetha could bend over a tub all day, scrubbing the nails from their fingers. God forbid that it should come to that!

Some time ago Armstrong's conduct had improved dramatically, for no apparent reason: he was more attentive and above all more patient. At first she was on her guard, expecting an outburst at any moment. But with the months she regained her confidence and sometimes even ventured to initiate a conversation on a subject about which she knew they had divergent views. Then came the news of his dismissal and a rapid deterioration in their relationship.

Gladys contemplated the bowl of rice in her hand, wondering at each grain, each a different shape, a different size and even a different hue, yet pressed together against one another in a bowlful. Then suddenly her hand lost its grip and the bowl fell to the ground and broke, scattering the grains across the floor. Instead of picking up the rice and the broken pieces she went into the children's bedroom and sank down on to their bed. She was feeling so badly that she lay on her side and experienced an almost irrepressible desire to shout for help. The thumping of her heart against her chest got worse, so she lay on her chest.

When she finally recovered she got the smelling salts bottle and applied it carefully to her nostrils. Who could live on twenty dollars a month? Was it possible that she was reduced to this? Long ago she took a cab whenever she went out, and in Agricola people called her "the lady". As she stepped out of her house, her parasol over her elegant molleed head they would look after her admiringly. Before she had married she wanted to have six children so that her house would be filled with light and laughter. Now she dared not look at herself in the looking-glass, lest the wreck with the rings round its eyes stare back at her. As girls she and her sisters loved to look through their father's binoculars, and their mother, irritated by their habit of holding the eye-piece at their eyes for long periods, often warned them: "You're going to get rings round your eyes you won't get rid of."

What if she took Boyie and Genetha and went home to her parents, at least for a few months? There they would eat well, there would be no housework, nor worry about leaking roofs, for her father, now manager of a large department store, seemed to be doing well.

But she could not entertain the dream for long; separation from Armstrong was unthinkable, and when he fell into the abyss the chain that bound their lives would drag her with him. She searched for a reason for this terrible liaison, but could not find one. Things were just so. There was a sky and an earth; there was the wind and the sun; and there was marriage.

She decided to get up and clean the kitchen floor, but found that she was unable to support herself. The giddiness and the heavy thumping returned, and as she tried to lift the smelling salts to her nostrils, the bottle fell out of her hand.

"Boyie!" she muttered, lowering her head gently on to the floor.

Doc paid for two lockers at the baths, changed and went outside to wait for Armstrong, who liked to spend a couple of minutes in the shower before going into the sea. He might have saved himself the trouble for rain had begun to fall and obscured the sea which was only about fifty yards away.

Turning round, Doc kept an eye on the single doorway of the long hutment from which bathers were emerging singly and in twos. Mostly teachers, he thought, believing he could recognise them "by the cut of their jib".

Odd that people seeing him and Armstrong in each other's company considered them close friends, Doc thought. Their heads were always together, yes, and their words exchanged in the certainty that they would be understood. But Armstrong had no idea how many things Doc hid from him, just as he discovered, with the opening of a single door that morning, a half of Armstrong he had heard speak of but had never seen, and whose dignity left him abashed.

Doc had never talked of the aboriginal Indian woman he had kept while teaching in the country and who had been the real cause of his banishment from the village and the threat of dismissal. That was the reason for his obsession with dismissal and his anxiety about his job. The aboriginal men isolated their women in huts for seven days of the month while they bled. Doc, who had been at that time associating with a charcoal burner, was introduced by him to one of them, a young, sidiom-skinned woman with feline eyes and a provocative gait, who did not mind lying naked in front of the hut while he gloated at her. He took her away to live with him in the village, parading her, scantily dressed, in the street under the hot sun. But his dream of living by instinct was cut short by a peremptory summons to visit the school manager's house.

Armstrong could not be relied on to accept this side of him, Doc thought. Therefore, he had told him about his wife, his *discipline*, as he described her, and with whom he could never achieve that roaring erection Taina called forth with a glance. Had it not been for Taina he would still have been yoked to his *discipline*.

Armstrong appeared at the door of the hutment, wearing one of the new short trunks fashionable among youthful bathers, an obscene invention that left little to the imagination, Doc reflected.

On seeing him Doc turned and made for the groin and

Armstrong promptly took off in pursuit, running into the wind with the exhilaration of friendship and the discovery, through his companion, of his good fortune in being married to Gladys.

They dived into the water, one followed by the other, and were soon swimming towards the open sea with the leisurely stroke of a crawl. Out they swam, in the wake of four-eyed shoals and the shrieking of shadowy gulls, smothered by the rain, till they had left the other swimmers behind and were alone among the grey, thundering waves.

The two men swam as in an effort to reach the limits of their understanding of each other, the secret behind their gestures, their affected carriage and guarded words. And the cruel thought occurred to Armstrong that B.A.'s fatal illness was the start of a deeper satisfaction in his relations with Doc. It was, as it seemed, the blood sacrifice essential to the flowering of a profounder frindship. When B.A. called out to them at the hospital that the two masked men who attacked him were of his and Doc's build, was he not right, in a way? Had not the same plan lurked in his, Armstrong's mind, taking care to clothe itself in moodiness when B.A. was late or made some untoward remark that bled his pride?

"I think we'd better go back," shouted Armstrong above the sound of the waves.

"Right," Doc answered.

And the two men turned and struck out towards the groin, barely visible in the rain.

Suddenly there was a piercing shriek and both men looked up to see a solitary gull wheeling in the rain. No other gull was in sight, while before scores had been diving and wheeling above them.

Armstrong was filled with foreboding. The single cry of the gull making wide circles in the rain, its head moving independently of its flight while it surveyed him and his companion, contained some momentous message, he was certain.

"You heard that?" he enquired of Doc.

"What? The bird?"

"Yes . . . hear how it screamed?"

"And what?" asked Doc.

Armstrong neglected to take the obligatory shower after leaving the salt, sea water. As Doc was going straight home anyway he bade him goodbye and hurried down the road, cursing himself for having come on foot.

He went past the slaughter house with its familiar sight of a line of black vultures perched on its roof and the reek of blood. And as he got further from the sea the wind fell, so that the rain no longer lashed his face.

Shoppers and others caught in the rain were sheltering under the corrugated iron awnings, like birds at roost. Every now and then Armstrong passed a carriage drawn by a pale brown horse with bedraggled head seeking the asphalt sheen and unmindful of its dejected master, whose whip was put away beside him.

"Damn it!" he thought, looking back at the carriage he had just passed. "I could have taken that one."

And now that he had resolved to hail a carriage the few that went by were occupied. There was no point in walking back to the cab-stand by the insurance company, for the distance home was now less than half a mile.

Anxiously he looked up to check the names of the streets he crossed, judging with each how far he must be from his house. Yet certain things came to his notice, the brick culvert and the only brick gutter he had ever seen in the town, and the brick pillars of a low-pitched house. And the observations of constructions in such an unusual material reinforced his foreboding.

Just before eleven, Armstrong returned home to find his wife on the floor, her face ashen grey and her hands dry as tinder. He knelt down and took her in his arms.

"Gladys, O my God! You're not going to leave me?"

But she could barely manage to ask to be taken inside. And holding her under her armpits he dragged her to the bed he had soiled more than once in sleeping with Marion.

Gladys could only mutter that she was feeling weak; but at his suggestion that he would fetch the doctor she grasped his hand and did not let go, muttering all the while that he must not.

"But your hands're so dry. . . . All right. When the children come home."

And when Boyie was heard chasing Genetha up the stairs, continuing a game begun in the street, Armstrong went out and told them to be quiet. He ordered Genetha to make her mother a cup of lemon grass tea and reminded her to be quiet when he was away in quest of the doctor.

The doctor, a pleasant old man who had forgotten most of his medical theory in the early years of his practice and had learned nothing new in the following years, professed to be perplexed. And on being asked by Armstrong what was wrong he said, "I'm not sure. I'll get a second opinion. Keep her warm and darken the room."

Armstrong gave the children bread and butter and cocoa and sent them out to play as soon as their meal was over, explaining that their mother was not well and needed all the sleep she could get.

In the afternoon the doctor came back with a colleague, who admitted to being as perplexed as he was.

And that night while the children were sleeping, Gladys Armstrong died. Armstrong, refusing to believe that his wife was no longer living, sat staring at the corpse.

After the rain, which had stopped falling about an hour ago, a profound silence had settled on the town, accentuated by the incessant dripping of water from roof gutters. Armstrong took his wife's hand in his. It was not possible that this hand that had grabbed his arm in the passion of their young love could feel like a dessicated leaf. Why had he not noticed before how pinched her face had become? Recalling the doctor's expression when he first examined her, Armstrong was ashamed that the signs of malnutrition should be so evident on her too-soon worn face.

No one could say that he had denied his wife and children food. With him his family had always come first. God was his witness! There were men who ate like hogs and let their people starve. That was not his way!

He got up and fumbled in the chest-of-drawers until he found an old photograph of himself and Gladys, taken soon after their marriage. He had his hands thrust in his pockets while she was holding on to his left arm and smiling in that way he would always remember her.

If only a man could see in the future and understand! She had never laughed at him when her sisters did, nor spoken to him with that suggestion of patronage that was her father's way. There had never been a suspicion of infidelity, no tantrums. . . . She had given him two healthy children. Was it possible that the same body that had urged him to face up to his responsibilities a short while ago should be but a shell? All the days and nights, the conversations by the window in Agricola, the carriage drives, the glances exchanged come to nothing! And the horn of his days was filled with dust! The children meant nothing to him, except as an expression of her life and of her presence.

Armstrong drew up a chair and sat down by the door of the room in which his wife lay, too bewildered to take any action.

The children would grow up and he would grow old, he reflected, and it was inconceivable that such momentous developments could occur without her, who gave birth to them, who had anchored him as a family man, supported him through the anguish of his dismissal and presented to him the mirror in which he discovered himself so painfully. Below him his sister was sleeping, no doubt deeply, unaware of the stilled voice. She was his blood, but he would have seen her die a thousand times than let his life's companion steal away, from him, from her children, from her possessions. . . . How strange! How strange life was! Around him was so much that was inanimate and so little that throbbed with life, only his children and himself, fluttering from day to day. And so much pain, as if pain was in the wind before it descended into the heart. Surely with a few more years his voyage of self-knowledge would have been complete and he would have been able to take her out into the bright afternoon sunlight of their declining years, arm in arm, to know again the happiness of their courting days. And over and over his thoughts travelled the same round of his past mistakes, as if by recalling them he could bring his wife back to life.

Despite the animosity between Gladys and himself over the years they had grown into each other like the hundred-year-old trees in the back yard, irrevocably entwined, and a matter of wonder to anyone who came visiting.

All of a sudden the thought occurred to Armstrong that his wife might not be dead at all. He dashed out of the house and ran all the way to the doctor's home, where he knocked hard on the door. The medical man, refusing to be hurried, walked with measured steps, Armstrong at his side.

After a cursory examination he pronounced Gladys dead and undertook to inform Mr Bastiani the undertaker.

"Pull yourself together. Think of the children!" he enjoined, annoyed that he had been dragged out of bed.

The next morning Armstrong's sister came upstairs to make the morning meal and to see that the children were prepared to go visiting, insisting that it was the best thing in the circumstances. Standing around the house would only distress them more.

"Do whatever you think necessary," Armstrong told Bastiani. "Give her a decent burial, but I leave the details to you."

Mr Bastiani was familiar with this attitude. Later on, when the realities of day-to-day living overcame the worst pangs of grief, the client would protest and make a show of refusing to pay. But they would see about that later. The problem now was to do the necessary for the corpse. A coffin of polished cedar, square glass panel above the head, purple lining, ornate metal handles and so on. . . . He would put Gittens on the job. Thank God death had come in the night! Convenient . . . very convenient, for that gave them time to work all morning. Pity everyone was not as considerate as that.

"Well, mustn't be too morbid," he thought, a smile lighting up his gaunt face.

Armstrong turned the pictures in the house towards the wall, as was the custom when there was a death in the house. He shut all the windows and the front door to keep out sympathisers, remaining in his bedroom for the rest of the day to brood on his bereavement; and only late that afternoon when the mourners' carriage arrived did he emerge from the house alone, forbidding the children to attend the funeral.

Alone in the carriage, which was moving at an unusually quick pace, recollections pressed on him, recollections of his children, his friends and of Lesney's dancing, as if thinking of his dead wife were unseemly. But as the carriage passed a gathering at a street corner — no doubt a religious meeting — his mind went back to the evening when, dressed in his best suit, he had stood on the edge of a crowd of people who were taking part in a Salvation Army meeting in Bourda. Carried away by the infectious singing and the sound of tambourines he forgot for a while that he was waiting to make his first visit to Gladys's house in Queenstown. He had set out too early and was obliged to wander around until he heard the music in the distance. No, her family would not have approved of tambourines or singing at street corners. Yet, such things stirred his heart. And these very things that separated them, these impulses, he suppressed for her sake, or perhaps for his own, believing that they were the signs of a defective upbringing.

The carriage turned right and, for the first time during the journey, he saw the undertaker's assistant on his cycle, leading the procession on a trip he made every afternoon. And behind him was the hearse pulled by a pale horse with strangely glowing mane.

From that evening with its resounding voices to this moment . . . a hearse with a gilded door, from the youth of her well-formed body to the emaciated remains there had been vouchsafed him a unique opportunity to raise a family successfully and die with dignity. For was not the family everything? Should he not have heeded the warning when he cursed his own father?

When the last spadeful of earth was thrown upon the grave he turned away and walked hastily up the path to the waiting carriage, along the avenue of eucalyptus trees that bordered the graves. He saw a group standing where two paths met and from among them emerged his father-in-law, who came up to him and pressed his hand in sympathy.

"Good luck!"

And as the old man walked away down the path Armstrong muttered, "Bugger you!"

The crowd of people went back to their carriages and cars, many of them glancing at him as they passed by the mourners' carriage, and his grief was replaced by a wave of anger at the sight of the well-dressed, well-spoken people, who had come to see his wife buried, but ignored his existence. It seemed to him that for them, it was as if Gladys had been married to a phantom which had managed to dress itself in mourning clothes for her committal to the other world.

And that same night, after the funeral, Armstrong stood by his wife's bedside. He must have loved her after all, for how else could he explain the feeling of desloation in his breast? Up to the day before, there had always been the certainty that she would be home when he came back home; that she would place before him the food he liked; that when he was in a bad mood she would tell the children to be quiet. In the presence of strangers she had been specially obliging and considerate. And what sort of life had he offered her? A wilderness of pain and anxiety.

He flayed himself with his remorse, and, in a fit of despair, began to weep silently. For a long time he kept his fingers over his eyes, as if he were being watched by onlookers before whom he was ashamed to display his grief. And the tears trickled through his fingers, down his chin to fall on to his shirt.

If only he knew how often she had sat in that self-same corner of their bed and wept as bitterly as he was doing. Boyie had more than once come over from the children's bedroom to ask her why she was crying.

Armstrong was roused by the water dripping into the bucket. He got up and went into the gallery to close the windows against the rain that had begun to fall again. The lamp post was gleaming under the light in the deserted street and the gate hung upon its single hinge, making a curious, short cry as it moved back and forth in the wind. The water, which had risen above the top of the street gutter, was rushing away noiselessly, covered with innumerable dots where the rain drops fell into it.

As Armstrong was about to close the Demerara window there appeared, in the middle of the street, a vision of a couple walking hand in hand. Her head rested on his shoulders as they ambled along, unmindful of the rain.

"I bet they're engaged," he thought.

As they approached he strained his eyes to see if the woman was wearing a marriage ring, and when they were quite near he bent forward to look at her left hand, which, however, bore no trace of a ring. He peered more closely to see their faces and shrank back in horror, for the man's face was deeply lined while she was equally aged, with soft, dark eyes. He recognised the two as himself and his dead wife and tried to grab the apparitions by the shoulder, only to see them vanish in the rain. Armstrong sank into a chair, trembling like a leaf.

The following day Armstrong's father-in-law came to see him and offered to take Genetha home for a few weeks or to keep her permanently with them, if Armstrong agreed. He consented to Genetha's stay for a few weeks, but no longer.

"Genetha!" Armstrong called out. "Come and talk to your grandfather. Ask him why he never came to see you all these years."

Genetha emerged from the back of the house and kissed her grandfather on the cheek. He had not seen the children at the funeral and wondered why they had not come; but this was not the time to ask.

"Where's your brother, Genetha?"

"He's probably playing at school," she answered, a little frightened of her grandfather.

"Don't you go with him to play?"

"No, I'm not allowed."

"Oh!" he exclaimed, not knowing what next to say to her. "Do you like school?"

"Yes," she replied untruthfully.

"Even when you have homework?" her grandfather asked, hoping that she would spin out her answers.

"No."

"What's one and one?"

"Two," she replied.

"Mm!" he exclaimed with feigned satisfaction.

She smiled and looked deep into his eyes.

"Are you good at your school work?"

"Only at English."

149

"All right, Genetha," he father broke in, "go inside and get ready."

Genetha dutifully asked to be excused and went inside, and when she came back her grandfather got up and took her by the hand.

"Call me 'Dad', like your aunts," he said, pinching her cheek between his thumb and first finger.

"Your tea's on the table, Father," she said.

Armstrong nodded, but made no effort to say goodbye to his daughter.

"I'll come again," declared his father-in-law, shaking his hand.

Armstrong got up and saw them both out, then went down the stairs and stood looking at them walk down the road hand in hand.

On the edge of a darkening sky were indigo islands, ablaze in the wake of a fallen sun.

Epilogue

It was I, it was I who killed him,
The serpent of Boropa
It was I who killed.
Then I was a child
All covered with buttons.
When the little girl sleeps
She puts her hand on her heart.

Brazilian song

Armstrong heard a noise on the bridge, got up and looked down through the jalousie. Catching sight of Doc he just had time to hurry into the bedroom without being seen. It was about eleven o'clock and he had already secured the windows for the night, but by some curious neglect had sat down before going to bed without having bolted the door. It was quite possible that Doc would take it into his head to open it and come searching for him.

The knocking was firm and when there was no answer came as near to pounding as a man's knuckles could make it.

"Armstrong! You're there?"

"If he wakes Boyie I'll have to open up for him," thought Armstrong.

"It's me! Doc!"

The knocking recommenced. But just as Armstrong was about to give in he heard the retreating footsteps on the stairs, then the footfalls up the deserted road.

Armstrong returned to his chair after bolting the door. He had not wanted Doc to find him in the mood he had been in all day, distraught and without counsel. When he recovered he would himself seek Doc out to find again those brighter days. And he would refrain from judging him, only remembering the need for companionship and hours of laughter. In the aftermath of his wife's death, black nights and mornings pale as clama-cherries, a kind of indefinable void. Only the day before, on his way to the market, hearing a burst of laughter behind him he turned round to discover who it was, but could see no one. A pale sun was shining from a sky scarred with clouds, and the ancient trees cast shadows across the canal dividing the two roads opposite the red-painted market. Once more the shrill outburst made him turn round. No living thing was there, not even a stray dog. There were no birds, no movement except the shuddering leaves of the giant trees. Then a man dressed in khaki shorts turned the corner from Orange Walk, ahead of Armstrong, who hurried onwards to seek the protection of his presence. On the way back home he took another road. As a boy he had heard his father say that he would never use a certain street; and, like everything else he said, it had seemed perverse to Armstrong at the time.

Armstrong wondered if his friend still went to Plaisance on Sundays, whether he would welcome an unexpected visit there as in the old days. He recalled that brilliant afternoon, his cantankerous "mother" and Baby, with her languid carriage. How long ago it seemed! How well-behaved everyone was then. In the last couple of years things seemed to have changed suddenly, and now you were liable to be knocked off the pavement by a youth learning to skate and be insulted into the bargain if you attempted to teach him a lesson for his brashness.

He went to bed with his thoughts and fell asleep to the high-pitched whirring of the cicadas.

The following afternoon Armstrong got dressed with the intention of visiting his in-laws. It was a few days after the New Year, the season of reconciliation. He put on his serge suit and black tie and at the last moment pinned on the black mourning-band to please Gladys's parents. The gesture would be lost on her eldest sister, but he was certain that her father would appreciate it.

There had been rumours that a new leader in Germany was seeking a war in Europe and this would provide a subject for conversation, which could occupy himself and his father-in-law for some time. He would not take his bicycle, which, for want of repair, was no longer suitable for a decent man.

Armstrong was adjusting his tie in front of the mirror when the front door closed noisily.

"The damn boy! He didn't even tell me he was going out; and his food's ready and all."

But the thought of seeing Genetha soon drove his son's unruliness out of his mind. Indeed, it was the idea that he and his daughter might grow away from each other that prompted him to make the visit. He suppressed his old rage against Gladys's family in the interest of his children, who should cleave to their grandparents and aunts, as was the case in most families.

Suddenly Armstrong was taken by a nameless anxiety. His blue serge suit, several years old but immaculate, appeared drab to him; his tie was the wrong colour and he found it difficult to align the mourning-band properly. Some indefinable

154

fear had scattered his thoughts so that he sat down on the bed and passed his hand over his face.

"What's wrong?" he asked himself aloud. "Dammit all! I only want to go and see my daughter. She is my daughter!"

He sprang up, tugged the mourning-band off his jacket and threw it on the bed. Without taking another look at his face in the looking-glass he strode out of the room and into the gallery, where he bolted the front door. After closing the back door — he left it unlocked in case Boyie should come home while he was out — he turned to descend the stairs. But he tripped on the second tread and fell forward. Desperately he grabbed the banisters of the back stairs and only just managed to hold on, his body stretched almost full-length across the treads of the steep staircase.

Badly shaken, Armstrong re-entered his house, seeing the accident as an omen. He went in search of a brush to clean his right shoe, which had scraped against the edge of one of the stair treads.

An indescribable weight seemed to bear down on him, causing his shoulders to droop and his defiant expression to vanish. Something was wrong, he reflected. But what? A mood? All of a sudden? From experience such moods disappeared once he ate something. Yet he had eaten only half an hour ago.

Gladys never approved of his superstitiousness, and he used to take care not to mention any such preoccupation to her. But the servants knew — and understood. God! After all he was from the country. And inevitably his thoughts turned to the gulf between himself and her family, an unbridgeable void that yawned between one way of life and another, like those mighty rivers that divide Amerindian tribes throughout the continent, as effectively as a high wall, and give rise to their own terrors. Armstrong recalled his father-in-law's manner when he asked Genetha in his presence why she thought he had not visited them all these years. He did not smile, did not seem put out in the least, did not even offer any reason for the neglect of his daughter or grandchildren. Could he not at least have said, "I thought that you disliked us, so we didn't come"? Nothing, not the slightest twitching in his features. And the renewed proof of his superciliousness, that certainty of status that was capable of overcoming even a crippled body or a devastating stammer, had driven Armstrong to distraction.

He decided against visiting, but visualised his arrival at the house in Irving Street, by way of Anira Street, just as at the time of his courting fourteen years before. There was the gate — the entrance — half-concealed beneath a growth of shrubs and flowers through which he used to pass in a kind of delirium. He always stopped under the house to take off his bicycle clips and adjust his jacket, to look around at the well-kept yard and marvel at the corrugated water-closet, one of the first to be built at the time of introduction of the sewage system in the early twenties.

Armstrong shook his head involuntarily and started undressing, when he suddenly called to mind his sister. A week ago he had found out where she was staying. If he were kind to her she would in all likelihood agree to come and live with them. Her last refusal had been made in a spirit of vengeance, and her character did not permit her to harbour a grudge.

Wasting no time he changed into more modest clothes, suitable for his mission.

She herself opened the door to him.

"It's you!"

"Yes. Do the people mind?"

"No, of course not. Sit down, ne. I'll just go in and tell them it's for me."

She looked well, he thought, disappointed that she was not as vulnerable as he had expected.

"You're all right here?" he asked, when she came out again.

"Yes. What about you and the children?"

"They're all right. Genetha is with her grandparents for a few weeks."

"And Boyie?"

"He's all right too. Looks as if he's enjoying secondary school."

"These people," he continued, "you know them well?"

"Oh, like that. Acquaintances more than friends."

"And they don't work you too hard?"

156

"No! I just have to be there and keep an eye on things when they're out. Do I look hard-pressed?"

"I didn't say so."

"Well, then," she said, lowering her voice to a whisper. "We can't always choose what we want. And as long as . . . as long as you're not unhappy."

"Did I say you were unhappy? You look well. And contented. Very contented. In fact when I came in I couldn't help noticing how contented you looked."

They talked of this and that, and all the while she wore a peculiar smile on her lips.

Judging that the right moment had come, he searched for something to say that might please her, but could find nothing.

"I want you to come and live with us . . . for my sake and the children's . . . and yours."

"I'm treated well here, Sonny. I want nothing," she answered, trying to hide her agitation.

"Do it for me then, and the children."

She reflected awhile.

"Will you give me Gladys's jewellery?" she asked, avoiding his eyes.

"There's nothing left," Armstrong answered. "Just a bangle."

"Only that?"

"We pawned everything."

"Give me the bangle then."

"If you want."

"And a share in your house?"

Armstrong cleared his throat and looked away. "All right; a share in the house too. Will you come?"

"No," replied his sister.

"But I thought," he protested.

"I'm not yet bitter," she said, as imperturbably as when the conversation began. "I'm still a young woman. D'you remember when I came for help in Agricola? Gladys was kinder than you. *She* became bitter."

"I forbid you to speak of Gladys!" Armstrong exclaimed angrily.

"Would you like a soft drink? The people I live with are very generous."

Someone turned on an electric bulb in one of the bedrooms and the light from it spilled over the low partition.

"So you won't help," he said, ignoring her offer of refreshment.

"I wish I could talk to you, Sonny. But you don't listen. I'm happy here, that's all."

"You keep on repeating that the people're generous and that you're happy," he said in exasperation. "But they're not family!"

The smile disappeared from her face and she looked at him unswervingly. She had died in puberty and then in her early thirties when it was certain that she would never marry. All her youth had been spent ministering to her father, whose death had brought Armstrong his freedom, but her a kind of enslavement to his memory. And now he, who had stolen her inheritance, came pleading with his two-mouthed words and talk of "family".

Armstrong's sister started to laugh softly. She sank her head in her right hand and laughed, laughed until no sound came. Her shoulders rose and fell convulsively and Armstrong, offended by her behaviour, got up from his seat and declared that he was going.

"Please don't come back," she said gently.

He left, angry, but aware of the danger of committing his past mistakes again. And as he went down the staircase, flanked by the painted balustrades, his sister looked up. Unknown to Armstrong she had been sobbing, above all because she had to dwell among strangers and depend on their hospitality. Yet, there was some satisfaction in living in a household in which the wife held sway and the husband knew his place.

Armstrong went in search of Esther in the main streets and by-ways. He even went up to Little Diamond, but her relatives knew nothing of her whereabouts. A shopkeeper suggested that he should insert an advertisement in the papers, which was bound to be spotted by one of her acquaintances. But the two pieces he paid for in the *Argosy* and *Daily Chronicle* brought no results. Odd it was that more than once he and the children had spotted Marion in town, threading her way between the stalls or standing in a cinema queue. But never Esther, as if she shunned public places.

So Armstrong came to terms with his life as it was. He was to bring up his children single-handed, having done what he could to enlist the assistance of someone close to the family. He had tried to visit his in-laws and could not get beyond his door-mouth. He had looked for Esther and was unable to find her. So he set out in quest of his wife under the eucalyptus trees that scattered raindrops like swarming butterflies, and stood in the thickening dusk watching the blown leaves and the pillow-stone. And looking down at her resting-place he meditated on his marriage and a child-big woman, on Doc and B.A. the seldom-pleasured friend, and on the years that spanned the twenties, a time, it seemed in retrospect, of plenty, when there was a rum-shop at every corner, and even immorality bore its flowers.

And Armstrong was overcome by a great calm that stilled the fears of Genetha growing away from him and his inability to handle his son. Then at the shout that the gates were closing he turned and left under a sky lit up at intervals by flashes of sheet-lightning, that announced the fullness of the rainy season.